CAVANAGH COWBOYS ROMANCE - 6

VALERIE COMER

Greenwords Media

First edition, GreenWords Media, 2022

Valerie Comer Bibliography

Farm Fresh Market Romance

1. A Wide and Pleasant Place

Urban Farm Fresh Romance

0. Promise of Peppermint (ebook only)
1. Secrets of Sunbeams
2. Butterflies on Breezes
3. Memories of Mist
4. Wishes on Wildflowers
5. Flavors of Forever
6. Raindrops on Radishes
7. Dancing at Daybreak
8. Glimpses of Gossamer
9. Lavished with Lavender
10. Cadence of Cranberries
11. Joys of Juniper
12. Together in Thyme

Pot of Gold Geocaching Romance

1. Topaz Treasure
2. Ruby Radiance
3. Sapphire Sentiments
4. Amethyst Attraction

Farm Fresh Romance

1. Raspberries and Vinegar
2. Wild Mint Tea
3. Sweetened with Honey
4. Dandelions for Dinner
5. Plum Upside Down
6. Berry on Top

Cavanagh Cowboys Romance
(Montana Ranches Christian Romance)

1. Marry Me for Real, Cowboy
2. Give Me Another Chance, Cowboy
3. Let Me Off Easy, Cowboy
4. Kiss Me Like You Mean It, Cowboy
5. Choose Me for Always, Cowboy
6. Trust Me With Your Heart, Cowboy

Saddle Springs Romance
(Montana Ranches Christian Romance)

1. The Cowboy's Christmas Reunion
2. The Cowboy's Mixed-Up Matchmaker
3. The Cowboy's Romantic Dreamer
4. The Cowboy's Convenient Marriage
5. The Cowboy's Belated Discovery
6. The Cowboy's Reluctant Bride

Garden Grown Romance
(Arcadia Valley Romance)

1. Sown in Love (ebook only)
2. Sprouts of Love
3. Rooted in Love
4. Harvest of Love

Miss Snowflake Pageant

1. More Than a Tiara
2. Other Than a Halo
3. Better Than a Crown

Riverbend Romance Novellas

1. Secretly Yours
2. Pinky Promise
3. Sweet Serenade
4. Team Bride
5. Merry Kisses

valeriecomer.com/books

CHAPTER ONE

Hey, thanks for coming to help. I thought for sure you would pick moving cattle over helping us get this grass planted."

Ryder Cavanagh shrugged as he grabbed a bottle of water from the back of his stepbrother's truck. "I've moved cattle a thousand times in my life, but I've never sown a lawn before."

"Me, neither." Nathaniel laughed. "I only hope the seed germinates somewhat evenly. I was all for getting a landscaping company to come in and lay sod, but Ainsley figured this way was better. Not to mention cheaper."

"I'm sure she's right." Ryder guzzled the water. It was excessively warm for late April in Montana, which gave him the excuse to remove his shirt while he worked. Hey, Nathaniel did it first, so why not?

Most of the brothers had broad shoulders and serious muscles, especially Noah, who was a blacksmith. Ryder was built more like Nat, though they weren't actually related. When they'd been kids, Blake had jeered at him and called him scrawny.

1

It had taken Ryder years to get over those taunts. Now, he preferred to think of himself as wiry.

Women doubtless favored built cowboys. The girls in Creekside Fellowship's youth group had always seemed to go for the bold, swaggering types and, since the blended Cavanagh clan had been home-schooled far from town, Ryder hadn't had a lot of other exposure to the fairer sex. Somehow his five older brothers had managed to escape Rockstead Ranch and meet the women of their dreams, but he lacked their confidence.

Coming up on twenty-five with no meaningful relationship? He couldn't blame it all on isolation. No girl could hold a candle to Carey Anderson, and she was off-limits.

Didn't keep a guy from hoping, though. Which was the precise reason he was down at Nathaniel and Ainsley's new house helping with the lawn. Ainsley and Carey were good friends, and maybe flexing his scrawny — no, wiry — muscles would get Carey's attention.

It was a stupid plan.

He glanced toward the house, but there was no one on the deck or visible through the windows. This was probably a total waste of time. Except for the grass. He parked his water bottle on the tailgate. "Ready for that last section?"

Nathaniel wiped his brow and resettled his cowboy hat. "Yep. You want to run the seeder or the roller this time?"

"Whichever." Ryder was easy.

"Grab the roller then." Nathaniel shook his head. "It's okay to have an opinion, bro."

"Doesn't matter."

Nat dumped a bag of seed into the drop spreader. "You may not want my advice…"

Nothing good could come from a sentence beginning like that.

"...but you're always holding back and taking the scraps, whatever someone else doesn't want. You don't have to be a bully and demand your own way every time, but it's okay to speak up once in a while, too."

"And here I thought easygoing was an art form." A movement at the window caught Ryder's attention, but he didn't look over.

Not when Nathaniel eyed him like that. "I worry about you."

"Don't." Ryder gave the roller an experimental back-and-forth. The thing was too light to show off his muscles. Whatever.

Half an hour later, he finished rolling the seed into firmer contact with the soil while Nathaniel emptied the spreader's hopper.

"Looking good, guys!" Ainsley called from the back deck. "Want some lemonade and cookies?"

"Do I ever *not* want lemonade and cookies?" Ryder cocked his eyebrow at Nathaniel's wife.

"You've got a point there, little brother. Come on in before you head back up to the ranch. Carey and I are just organizing things in the kitchen cupboards. I can't wait to be completely moved in. This house is amazing."

Ryder's heart hitched at the mention of Carey's name, but he ignored it. He thumbed over his shoulder toward the other brand-spanking-new house next door. "Travis and Dakota finished moving in, right?"

"Last week." Nathaniel set his cowboy hat on the tailgate and tugged his T-shirt back on over his head.

Ryder supposed he should do the same. He'd rather have a

quick shower before coming near Carey. She likely wouldn't appreciate the smell of sweat.

Nathaniel hooked his arm around his wife's waist and twirled her in for a long kiss.

So, maybe perspiration wasn't an automatic turnoff.

Ryder shrugged into his snap-front shirt before glancing toward the house again.

Carey stood in the doorway, her shoulder-length brown hair pulled into a ponytail that left wisps around her face. Her pink T-shirt and shortish floral skirt looked amazing on her slim build, and pink toenails gleamed from her bare feet.

His gaze met her brown eyes. Ugh, she'd caught him perusing her. He managed a smile. "Hey, Carey."

"Hi, Ryder."

A crash sounded from inside, followed by a piercing wail. Carey pivoted and darted off half a step ahead of Ainsley, who'd needed to disentangle from Nathaniel first.

"Bella!" Ainsley screamed. "Oh, no. Don't move!"

Ryder dashed into the house on Nathaniel's heels. The sobbing three-year-old stood in the middle of a puddle surrounded by broken glass, ice cubes, slices of lemon, and sprigs of mint.

A newborn echoed the crying from the other end of the house.

Nathaniel plucked his daughter out of the mess. "You okay, sweetie?"

Ainsley wrung her hands. "I can't believe she tried to pour the lemonade. I can't believe I turned my back on her for five seconds. I can't believe—"

"Shh. She's not hurt, love. I think she was too frightened to take a step."

"But she could have stepped on the broken glass! I should have—"

"It's okay." Nathaniel shifted Bella to one arm then pulled Ainsley to his side. "I bet she won't do that again, will you, baby?"

With a hiccupping sob, the little girl leaned her curly head against her daddy's shoulder and tucked her thumb in her mouth. Nathaniel's hand nearly covered Bella's small back as he rubbed it.

Ryder dared breathe. That could have been a lot worse. The heavy pitcher could have dropped on her head and given her a concussion. A lemonade shower was a small price to pay.

Ainsley darted off, and the infant's cry shushed, too.

Nathaniel met Ryder's gaze. "I'll be back in a minute. Just going to get Bella cleaned up and make sure she's not hurt."

"Don't worry about a thing." Ryder waved his hand. "I've got this."

"Thanks, bro." Still carrying Bella, Nathaniel strode down the hallway.

Being a husband and father of two suited Nat to a tee. Would Ryder ever get the chance to experience those things himself?

When the bathroom door clicked shut, Ryder turned to survey the mess he'd promised to mop up.

Carey already squatted on the other side, picking up shards and dropping them into the somewhat-intact pitcher base.

His heart lurched. "You shouldn't be in there with bare feet. I don't want you to step on any glass."

She glanced up at him. "I'm being careful. Besides, I think

I've got most of it already." She began to stand, wobbling a little as she noticed another shard and stretched for it.

Ryder didn't stop to think. He simply reached for her to keep her from falling. But, oh. Touching her felt good.

CAREY NEARLY STOPPED BREATHING as Ryder's strong hands caught her flailing ones and kept her from tumbling seat first into the puddle of lemonade. Wouldn't that be undignified, especially in a skirt! She only wanted to prove she was no damsel in distress who would stand by and wring her hands while watching a guy clean up such a big mess.

She was probably as much to blame as Ainsley for leaving the toddler in the same room as temptation. After all, didn't Bella adore lemonade? Hadn't she perched on the counter and clapped gleefully as every citrus slice dropped to the bottom before floating upward again?

But now, here Carey was, both wrists caught in Ryder's grasp as he helped pull her to standing. The cowboy had amazing deep blue eyes. She'd never noticed them quite like this before. She'd only watched him from a distance, because there was no way a guy like him would be interested in a girl like her.

His gaze still holding hers, he loosened his grip. "You okay now?"

"Yes. Thanks." If only she didn't sound so breathy, like a vapid female fanning herself in a Regency romance. Her wrists felt a little chilled without his touch, which was all kinds of weird since it must be nearly eighty degrees in here.

"All right." Ryder took a step back.

So did Carey, but a piercing pain dug into her heel.

"Ouch!" She tried to rebalance, get some clear footing, but a slippery lemon slice seemed to be under her other foot.

She was going down.

Except Ryder caught her again, this time swooping her all the way into his arms as the broken pitcher dropped and tipped, some of the shards tumbling back out onto the tile.

"Are you all right?"

He was so close she could smell the sweat on his body from the honest work he'd been doing with Nathaniel. But she could also smell the scent of his aftershave and the mint of his breath.

"Sorry I'm so clumsy."

He grinned. "I've got you."

"You sure do." Carey stared back.

Ryder cleared his throat. "Here, let me put you down on a barstool and have a look at your foot. And then you just stay put while I get this cleaned up. I've got boots on. I'll be fine."

Who was she to argue? "Okay."

He deposited her gently on a tall stool then squatted in front of her, his strong warm hands angling her foot so he could see the bottom. "Looks like just the one bit." He flicked it away. "If you feel more, I'll ask Ainsley for a pair of tweezers, but I think you're good."

"Thanks."

Ryder searched her face for a few seconds.

What was going through his mind? She had no idea. It drove her crazy, because she never could tell with him. Every once in a while, she thought for sure he was interested in her, but then he never said anything, never made any movement in that direction, so she was certain she imagined it. But it happened just often enough — every few months — that she kept wondering.

It was kind of ridiculous, actually. She was a grown woman of twenty-eight, a physical therapist at a great clinic in downtown Jewel Lake. She shouldn't be pining away after a man who was several years younger than she was, especially not the stepbrother of her cousins. That practically made Ryder family, no matter how much she tried to convince herself otherwise.

In the twenty-first century, it was perfectly fine for a woman to make the first move. Of course, her maternal grandmother would turn over in her grave at the very thought of such impropriety, but it was all Granny Wilson's fault for not doing a better job of hiding her stash of Georgette Heyer novels. Carey had been heartbroken after her parents' divorce and having to start over in a new neighborhood and school in Missoula. She'd discovered Granny's bookshelf at a rather impressionable age, and the escape into another time and world had been a healing balm.

Granny had been horrified when she discovered Carey tucked up with *Cotillion*, dreaming that, like Kitty Charing, a rich, handsome suitor would fall in love with her. The shelf in Granny's room had emptied overnight, but by then Carey had a library card and kept reading until she'd exhausted every one of the Queen of Regency's novels she could find.

She watched as Ryder used half a roll of paper towel to gather the mess, dropping the saturated wads into the trash can. He was nearly done when she heard Ainsley's voice coming nearer.

Carey should probably be down on the floor helping, but hadn't Ryder given her strict orders? Far be it from her to upset the guy, even though he didn't seem to have the temper some of his family was reputed to have.

"Oh, Ryder!" Ainsley stopped in the doorway holding two-week-old Oakley. "I'm so sorry you felt you had to clean all that up."

"No prob, Ainsley." He shot his sister-in-law an easy grin. "Is Bella okay? Carey stepped on a little piece of glass, but I think she's good now."

"Bella's fine. Nathaniel is giving her a bath." Ainsley's gaze found Carey's. "And you got cut?"

"I'm really fine. Ryder took care of it, just like he's taking care of the rest of it." She couldn't even be bitter about being sidelined. Wasn't that what a gentleman was supposed to do?

"I just need a bucket of soapy water now." Ryder set the diminished roll of paper towel on the counter across the room. "Before your new tiles dry all sticky."

"You're amazing, Ryder." Ainsley stretched to give her brother-in-law a little peck on the cheek. "Thank you."

Red bloomed across his face as he shot a teensy glance at Carey. "Glad I could help."

"I don't even know where a bucket is. I can't believe my baby brain." Ainsley wrung her hands. "Did we unpack cleaning supplies yet, Carey?"

"Hall closet. I'd get it myself, but I have strict orders..." Carey gestured to her feet. They were nearly as sticky as the floor. "If someone would bring me warm water, I'd love to wash, and then I can help."

"I'll get that for you." Ryder pivoted toward the hallway.

"What got into him?" Ainsley frowned, jiggling Oakley. "He's acting all weird."

No way was Carey going to express her opinion on that one because, just this once, it seemed as though Ryder saw her. For real.

CHAPTER TWO

I can't believe your wife let you get away for a few days of fishing." Ryder shifted in Champlain's saddle and glanced back at the two packhorses moseying along behind him and Blake.

Blake flashed him a grin. "She knows I need my nature time. Besides, Vivienne is staying with her and Gavin. It sounded like there would be a lot of chick flicks happening around the condo in the evenings."

"Poor Gavin." Though the seven-year-old went to bed fairly early, at least on school nights.

"I know, right? I'll bring him up to the trappers cabin for the weekend sometime after all the snow has melted. He loves fishing, but he has no meat on his bones to keep him warm, and his attention span is short."

Ryder laughed. "You love the kid, but sometimes you need a break."

"Sometimes I need a guy trip. You'd better be old enough that I don't need to worry about every move you make."

"I think so. I might fall off a log and put you to the test, just to keep you watchful."

"Very funny."

"Dafne's okay with you coming home with a stringer of trout? She's such a city girl."

"City girl turned cowgirl." Blake looked over with a grin. "I think it proves God's got a sense of humor."

"You got that right."

"When are you going to find yourself a woman and settle down?"

"Like any of you were married at my age." Ryder couldn't keep his mind from drifting to Carey. She was the same age as several of his sisters-in-law. Friends with them.

"It's not a rule. But you might have to go into town once in a while to meet someone."

"Not my scene. Not like you played it, anyway."

Blake grimaced. "Okay, so I wasn't the smartest cowpoke in the West. But it all worked out in the end."

"I'll get there someday." At least, Ryder hoped so. Not that he could talk to any of his brothers about his unrequited love for Carey Anderson. Of course, it wasn't actually love. More like a fixation. An infatuation. An addiction. Ryder had never been in love, so he wouldn't know the difference.

"Right?"

Ryder blinked as he refocused on his brother. "Pardon me? I must have missed something."

"You were gazing off with a smirk on your face. Don't tell me that wasn't about a girl."

A smirk? More like a grimace, probably, no matter what it looked like to Blake. "There isn't anyone in my life. You know that."

"But you wish there were."

"Well, sure. Seems pretty clear from the Bible that God didn't mean for a man to stay solo all his life."

"Trust you to bring God into it." Blake scanned the trail ahead of them before looking back at Ryder. "What do you think God wants us to do about our mother?"

"You're asking me? I haven't seen her since your wedding. Which *you* must have invited her to."

"Did not. She must have heard about it and just showed up. It's not like we were trying to keep any big secrets. It honestly never crossed my mind that she'd figure she had a right to be there. Ugh. What a scene she made."

It had been months ago now, and they hadn't heard from her since Kathryn, bless her heart, had escorted Mom home that night.

"Maybe I should elope like Noah did. Then she wouldn't find out ahead of time and crash it."

"Still can't believe Noah did that. He'd never done an impulsive thing in his life."

"Yeah, it was pretty shocking." Ryder had figured he'd have warning before suddenly becoming the last Cavanagh brother standing. But, no. Just when it had become apparent Noah and Taryn had completely fallen in love, they'd just up and eloped a few weeks after Blake and Dafne's wedding. That had been last summer, and the newest newlyweds seemed blissfully happy.

"But I probably should have reached out to Monica before that happened. Seeing Dafne with Gavin... a mother's bond with her son can be pretty intense."

"Our mother abandoned us, so the bond obviously wasn't that strong." Ryder had only been five. He didn't have a lot of memories from back then, but he did remember being heartbroken and bawling his eyes out night after night with no one to tuck him in bed. Dad sure hadn't taken over the nurturing. Nor had Travis or Blake. The household had been full of anger-laced testosterone.

His next memory was of Kathryn snuggling him, becoming a mommy to a little kid who needed one. She'd brought a measure of gentleness to the house, but she'd also brought three more boys, and Ryder had felt nearly as lonely in the crowd as he had when his own mother left.

"I think Monica regrets it," Blake mused.

Ryder wasn't so sure. "How do you figure that?"

"Not leaving Dad, I don't think. You probably don't remember how much they yelled and swore and threw heavy objects at each other. Their marriage was pretty unsustainable, and I think we're lucky it didn't end with either of them in jail for assault or murder."

"I have some vague memories." Ones he tried to squelch.

Blake shuddered. "Be thankful if that's all. But I think she regrets leaving us boys behind and not keeping contact."

"I'm glad she did. As harsh as Dad was at times, I'm glad I got to grow up at Rockstead instead of wherever she went off to."

"Yeah. Me, too." Blake's mouth twisted to one side as he thought. "Just saying that seeing Dafne with Gavin gives me a whole different perspective than I ever had before. Seeing a little boy who didn't have a dad is different than us kids without a mom."

"But we had Kathryn."

"We have to give her credit for trying, huh? Dad's so impossible."

"I think he's softening some," Ryder ventured.

"You think?" Blake studied him. "It's hard to tell. Seems the same to me, for the most part. Maybe a little quieter."

"I've had him to myself at breakfast and dinner all winter." Times when Ryder definitely missed all his older brothers, who no longer lived at the ranch since they were all married. Thankfully, they were often present at the lunch table.

"So, tell me."

"He doesn't yell as much."

Blake snorted. "Because you're not the rebel Travis or I were. You just take whatever he dishes out."

Protest was futile, because Blake wasn't completely wrong. Ryder didn't figure a guy needed to rock the boat simply to prove he could. "He and Kathryn have been seeing a counselor in Missoula."

"Really? I heard that but figured he probably only went once or twice."

Ryder shook his head. "No. At least half a dozen times now. Emma corroborates that from Kathryn's side."

"The girls still show up often on weekends? I kind of miss them."

"They do, on Sunday afternoons, anyway, since Viv has that day off from retail." Ryder glanced at his brother. "Vivienne should have a horse of her own."

"You know, that's a good idea. Ideally, that should come from Dad, but it doesn't look like he'll ever get around to it. Does she want one?"

"I'm not sure. She doesn't visit much, but that's probably more on Dad than the lack of her own horse."

Blake snorted. "It's been nearly two years. If he were going to act like her father, he'd have started by now."

"But the counseling has only been going on for a few months." Ryder hesitated. "I could ask him about a horse for Viv."

"You're braver than I gave you credit for."

"I should resent that."

"But you're too easygoing to bother."

If only his brothers knew how *not* easygoing Ryder felt at times. But it wasn't like he knew what else to do with his emotions besides shove them aside.

The horses plodded on up the trail, the air cooling and the snowdrifts deepening as they gained altitude. Ryder relaxed a bit, inhaling the mountain breeze. With conversation on pause, he could hear the occasional bird flitting in the canopy. They'd be to the cabin in another half hour or so, where they'd divert the stream into the holding tank, start a fire in the cookstove, and unroll their sleeping bags in the loft.

Cook had sent enough grub for four guys, but then, they always went through a lot when they worked in the high ranges. Sure, they'd be fishing much of the time, but they'd be cutting wood to replace what had been used over the winter, too. A guy never knew when someone might be stranded in the high country and need a ready shelter.

"Are you still working on that whole thing about Jason Anderson? I haven't heard anything about it in eons."

Ryder turned in his saddle to look at his brother. "Do you think I should?"

"Are you, or aren't you?" Blake rolled his eyes.

"Branson's been busy with his studies, so I haven't pushed it lately."

"He's, what, wrapping up his third year of law school now?"

"Fourth." Branson deWitt had been in youth group with Ryder a few years back. Both loners, they'd found a bit of comfort in hanging out at the fringes of the group together. Ryder had confided in his friend when oddities had begun coming to light about his stepbrothers' uncle, Jason Anderson, and the insurance he'd tried to sell Joe. Seemed Jason had really wanted to get his hands on Running Creek Ranch and didn't much care about his brother's grieving widow and sons.

The man had disappeared a while back. Maybe Carey or her sister knew where their father was, but if they did, Ryder hadn't heard. He also hadn't asked.

"Kathryn doesn't seem concerned about pursuing Jason. If he'd wronged her, wouldn't she be pushing for justice?"

Ryder considered Blake's words. "I don't know. She spent so many years barely surviving marriage to our father, I don't think she had the energy or mental space to delve into all that."

"I hate to say it, but she seems to be doing much better without Dad."

Ryder scrunched his nose. "I don't think it's the 'without Dad' bit so much as having re-entered society. She really likes teaching and having friends around her. Plus, the twins keep her on her toes in town."

"You should take a page out of her book. Maybe you'd do well with friends, too. Even a girlfriend."

"Funny guy."

"I thought so." Blake smirked. "But back to Jason. I think it would be a good idea to follow through with what you've started, just so we can set it aside. I doubt there's anything worth prosecuting, but I could be wrong."

"Wait, did you really just say that?"

"What, that I could be wrong? It's happened a time or two, or so Dafne tells me."

"It's like you really *have* grown up."

"You, too, could grow up just like me. You should be so lucky."

Ryder couldn't squelched the snort that escaped.

"Too bad Daf doesn't have a kid sister, but she has a few cousins we could introduce you to."

"Not a chance." Ryder held up his hand. "No city girls for me, thanks."

"It's kind of fun introducing one to rural life. When Dafne gets scared, she clings to me." Blake hiked his eyebrows.

"Ugh, that's more information than I needed. She's great. I'm glad for you, but that's not what I'm looking for."

"A cowpoke like you can't be so picky."

"What's that supposed to mean? I could be like Noah and pick up a runaway bride on the side of the road. Adam practically did the same thing, come to think of it."

"They both had to get off the ranch to do it, though. Same with Nathaniel and Travis and me. You need to get into town more, bro."

"Travis doesn't count. He and Dakota knew each other since they were like twelve."

"I'll give you that one. But they still met in town, not at Rockstead." Blake gestured to the mountain peaks in the distance. "Not way back here in the high country."

"I'll meet her someday. I'll know her when I see her."

Blake gave him a studying look. "Maybe you've met her already."

"Maybe." Ryder kept his voice casual. "Who knows?"

"You said you'd know when you saw her, so if you've met her… you already know."

"You're quite the literalist." But Ryder's heart rate had picked up speed. Because he *had* met her, and he *did* know. He was simply trying to undo the knowing, because it was completely pointless.

His dream of a relationship with Carey would be even

more futile if he managed to pin anything prosecutable on her father. So… why not just let the investigation die off? Branson hadn't mentioned anything since he'd been home at Christmas break, and Ryder hadn't reminded his friend. There wasn't that much of a trail. Yeah, Jason had been sleazy back in the day, but Kathryn had sidestepped the dude. All was well that ended well, right?

Dad had finally ceded Running Creek Ranch back to Kathryn's sons. That's where Adam and Riley and their eleven-month-old son, Joseph, lived now. But they'd all agreed to operate the two spreads as one business.

Jason had failed at whatever he'd been trying back in the day. Maybe there wasn't any need to dig into ancient history. Jason's brother Joe's family had landed on its feet, after all.

Leaving it alone would be one less thing keeping Ryder from pursuing Carey.

But it still wouldn't be enough, because nothing could make him older than her or remove the relationships between their families.

CHAPTER THREE

I ran into your old boss today. He'd sure love to have you back."

Carey shifted the phone to her other ear, hoping she'd hidden her involuntary sigh at Laurel's words. "I like it here."

"You said yourself that your friend moved out to the ranch, so she's not even nearby anymore. Plus, isn't she busy with her new baby?"

"It's true, but Ainsley wasn't the only reason I came back to Jewel Lake." Why couldn't her sister give up? It wasn't that they'd hung out much when they'd lived in the same building complex in the city.

"Right. Because you like people associating you with Dad."

"Of course not. But he moved away a long time ago, too."

"Not everyone has forgotten Jason Anderson. Someone was asking me about him just the other day."

"See? You live in Missoula and can't avoid it. No one has mentioned him to me in ages."

"This guy — Branson deWitt — do you know him?"

"Seems like there are deWitts in town, but the name Branson isn't ringing a bell."

"Hmm. He was looking for Dad's current address. Like I'd give it to some random guy who walked in off the street."

Carey shifted uneasily. "How did he find you? There must be hundreds of Andersons in Missoula."

"I know, right? And this guy was young, so he wasn't a crony of Dad's from back in the day."

"Maybe he's our long-lost brother." Carey couldn't keep the bitterness out of her voice. She and Laurel had pretended they didn't know Dad was keeping other company when they were little, but it had been impossible to avoid when their parents' marriage had exploded. Mom had thrown all kinds of accusations in Dad's face. Yeah, she'd apologized to the girls later for what she'd said in front of them, but that hadn't restored their innocence.

"I wish that wasn't an actual possibility."

"Right?" Carey shook her head. "I don't know what Dad was thinking, messing around so much."

"You and me both, sister. At least Mom's doing all right. She and Frank make a good team."

"They do. I'm glad she got over Dad." Carey wished she could do the same.

"She got to change her name when she married Frank. That's about the best reason I can think of to get married."

"You can change your name legally without, you know."

"I've been tempted, trust me." Laurel sighed. "We could do it together? Unless you're hiding a diamond ring and are planning to ditch the Anderson name the old-fashioned way."

"No diamond. No engagement, hidden or otherwise. No boyfriend, in fact."

"We're a sad pair."

There wasn't much to add. Her sister was right.

"We should both quit our jobs and move somewhere far away together. Like California."

Dad had moved East. It didn't escape Carey's notice that her sister dreamed of the opposite direction. "I'm not going anywhere."

Laurel huffed a laugh. "There must be a guy then."

No, just a vague daydream about one lean cowboy whom Carey could never have. He wouldn't make the first move, nor would she. There were too many reasons, propriety notwithstanding.

She did think Ryder felt something for her, the way he'd looked at her when he'd brought her the bucket of warm water that day at Ainsley's. But that had been a couple of weeks ago, and she hadn't seen him since. Which pretty much corroborated her own theory, that a little mild attraction between them wasn't enough to offset their family connection and age difference.

"Did I lose you?"

Carey dragged her thoughts back to Laurel. "No. I'm here. Still no guy."

"Come into town on Friday and have dinner with me at the restaurant?"

"Not this week. I'm going over to Ainsley and Nathaniel's."

"It's like she's your sister instead of me."

Actually, it was like Ainsley had fewer expectations than Laurel did. Laurel spent all her time dissecting their father. Carey wanted to forget he existed. Sure, she'd moved back to the town they'd lived in when she was a little kid — when she and Ainsley had first been friends — but after the first round of 'you must be Jason and Ellen's daughter,' people had turned to what she was doing now. She worked at Lakeside Sports

Therapy, helping athletes and others recover from injuries or surgeries. She'd done the same in Missoula, but here there were more cowboys.

Only one, in her eyes.

A knock sounded at Carey's door, which was weird, since no one had buzzed to be let into the building. "Listen, Laurel, I've got to go."

"Okay, fine. Whatever. Come see me soon, and we'll do dinner."

"Or you could visit here. The Golden Grill is as amazing as it ever was." She hurried toward the door. "You used to love their cheesecake."

"I'd get fat eating there often."

Carey peered through the peephole to see one of the Cavanagh twins standing there. She opened the door. "Hi, Emma!"

"Hey. Um, can I borrow a cup of sugar?"

"Sure. Come on in. Laurel, I've got to go. Talk to you later." She tapped to end the call and set her cell on the corner of the kitchen counter. "Sorry. That was my sister. I'm sure you know how that goes. They talk your ear off all the time and think they know what's best for you. Am I right?"

"Yeah. Lex is like that, too."

Carey opened her cupboard and pulled down her vintage sugar canister. "Did you bring a bowl or container?"

"Um, no. I can't believe I forgot. Sorry."

Strange conversation. "Okay. Why don't I put it in a zip bag then?"

"Thanks. That sounds good." Emma watched as Carey found a snack-size bag.

"So, what are you making? Cookies?"

"Vivienne wants to bake a gingerbread cake."

"I'm surprised your mom is out of sugar." Carey might be wrong — she apparently *was* wrong — but Aunt Kathryn always seemed so organized and together. She simply didn't seem the sort to not be well stocked, even though Carey could attest that the apartments in this building didn't contain much storage space. That must be it, although Kathryn's place had three bedrooms and Carey's only one. However, she'd forgotten to add something important to her grocery list more than once, herself. She could see how it could happen. "Gingerbread cake sounds delicious. Not everything has to be about chocolate all the time."

Emma accepted the baggie. "Thank you. I'm not sure I agree, though. Isn't chocolate life?"

Carey chuckled. "Most women seem to think so. But I'll let you in on a little secret. Cocoa makes me break out. Every single time. So, while I love the taste of it, it doesn't really love me back."

"Huh. That's weird. You should come over later and have a piece. Viv says it's a recipe her mom used to make all the time."

"Maybe I will." At least, if her aunt invited her. Carey wasn't sure if she should accept the teen's overture as official.

Emma flashed her a shy smile. "Please do. See you later, and thanks again."

Carey watched the girl scurry down the carpeted corridor and into the stairwell. She'd kind of hoped when she took an apartment in this building that she'd have occasion to randomly run into Ryder. At the time, she hadn't been thinking of the fact that Kathryn was his stepmother, not his mom, so he probably didn't come by often.

Maybe Laurel was right. It was kind of silly to stay living in Jewel Lake in the hopes that someday Ryder Cavanagh would notice her. Problem was, she didn't have a better reason to live anywhere else.

"THANKS, kid. It's not every day someone invites me for cake." Ryder nudged Alexia's arm with his elbow. "It's not even my birthday."

"Don't be fooled, Ryder." Kathryn chuckled. "What they really want is a ride up to the ranch later. Vivienne has to work tomorrow, and these two have suddenly decided their mares are dying of loneliness without them."

He eyed the twins. "Does Dad know you're coming?"

Alexia tossed her head. "Who cares? He ignores us, anyway. And Cook always makes our favorites when we're there. It's no skin off his back."

Ryder wasn't so sure springing a visit on their father was such a great idea, but maybe they were right. They'd be a little buffer at dinnertime, at least. The girls never came downstairs for breakfast at seven, but they were right about Cook. She'd spoil them, either way. She'd done so ever since they'd been born.

He couldn't blame the woman who'd managed the ranch kitchen since he could remember. She definitely wasn't the only one who'd catered to every whim of that pair of babies. Everyone had been happy back then, with the possible exception of Travis and Adam, whose intense rivalry had started young. The rest of them doted on their sisters and assumed happy times were there to stay.

Yeah. That hadn't happened.

"Is Carey coming?" Alexia turned to Emma.

"Not sure." Emma shrugged. "Maybe she'll come if Mom tells her we're ready now."

Ryder managed to keep his eyes from narrowing. Why had they invited Carey? Not that he minded — quite the opposite — but it still seemed strange.

"Sure, I'll call." Kathryn reached for her cell. "Hi, Carey? Emma mentioned she'd borrowed sugar from you and invited you for cake. We're serving in a minute, so if you're free, come on up ... sure, sounds good."

"I... do you need a hand with anything?" No way could he sit on the sofa like a frog on a log while waiting for a knock at the door.

"How are you at whipping cream?" Vivienne eyed him.

He shrugged. "Never tried it, but I know I love eating it."

"Guys." She rolled her eyes.

"You didn't miss much, growing up without brothers," Alexia grumbled at Viv. "I was going to whip the cream."

Ryder wrapped his arm around Alexia's neck and gave her a noogie on her skull. "Show me how?"

She ducked under his arm. "You seriously don't know?"

"How would I? I'm a cowboy. When would I have learned to whip cream?"

"You said you like eating it."

"What I really meant was that I like squirting it right from the can into my mouth. I assume that's not what we're talking about here."

"Ugh." Alexia shuddered. "Mom!"

Kathryn chuckled. "He's not too old to be taught. Just make sure he doesn't turn it into butter."

Emma grabbed Ryder's arm and dragged him toward the kitchen.

"Mmm, I like butter almost as much as I like whipped

27

cream. Maybe more." He allowed himself to be hauled along.

"Don't. Even."

"What?" He put on an air of innocence, which was almost the same as ignorance, right? And that was easy, since he really didn't have a clue. "Is it actually that easy to make butter?"

"Mom!" yelled Alexia. "He's impossible."

"I haven't heard the mixer start," Kathryn called back. "Don't give up on him yet."

There was a knock at the door. Ryder's heart sped up, but he wouldn't check to see if it were Carey. He surveyed the kitchen with its dusting of flour and eggshells and dollops of brown batter on the counter. Vivienne was pouring hot water into the sink. Maybe he should volunteer to clean up and let the girls do the cream, after all. He could hardly make the mess worse. Hadn't he succeeded at cleanup at Nat and Ainsley's a couple of weeks ago?

The last time he'd seen Carey.

"Thanks for inviting me, Aunt Kathryn. Gingerbread cake sounds so delicious. I don't think I've ever had that before."

Ryder forced himself not to turn back into the front room and gaze on Carey's beautiful face. "What do I do?" he asked his sisters.

"Here." Emma poured a pint of cream into a stainless-steel bowl while Alexia snapped two whisks into the handheld mixer and plugged it in. "Turn it on. Make sure to keep the beaters in deep, so it doesn't spatter all over."

"I can do that." He found the *on* button. Thankfully, it made just enough noise that he couldn't hear Kathryn and Carey talking in the other room.

How could Ryder have guessed that accepting this invitation meant seeing Carey? Surely his sisters hadn't picked up on his feelings for their cousin. See, that's what was wrong with this whole thing. The relationships were too close.

But *he* wasn't related to her, just because his sisters were.

Ugh. Complicated.

"Hey, Ryder! I see they've put you to work."

He pivoted, knocking the beaters against the edge of the bowl. It skittered sideways to the edge of the counter.

"Hey!" Alexia yelped, grabbing it a second before disaster would have struck. As it was, blobs of whipping cream flew every direction.

Emma pressed the *off* button, and the whisks stopped spinning.

Still, it was too late to keep him from looking like a bumbling idiot. "Uh, hi, Carey."

"I'm sorry I startled you."

Emma took the mixer out of his nerveless fingers. "I'll finish. Get out of here before you wreck something for real. I don't know why we even let you in the kitchen."

"Hey! I want to learn how to do this."

"Out." Alexia pressed both hands against his back and pushed him right past Carey and into the living room.

"But..." Ryder tried to dodge his sister and return to his task.

Carey grinned at him from just inside the kitchen, her brown eyes twinkling. "You've got a bit of whipped cream right here." She swiped a finger across his cheek.

His entire face tingled. Maybe it was mostly from embarrassment. He should just accept his humiliation. He would, if it weren't for the way her gaze lingered on him.

"That's not the only place." Alexia got between them with a damp cloth and dabbed at his denim snap-front shirt. "Stay out of the kitchen, Ry."

CHAPTER FOUR

I didn't know such amazingness existed." Carey squished the last few decadent crumbs beneath her fork and popped them in her mouth. "I can't thank you enough for inviting me, and I do hope you'll share the recipe with me."

Vivienne glowed under her praise. "Sure. It's a cake my mom used to make often. Ainsley always preferred chocolate, but this one was my favorite."

"I can see why. The flavor is so rich and deep."

"Carey said chocolate makes her break out," Emma announced casually.

Thanks, kid. This wasn't something Carey would announce in front of a guy, especially Ryder. She'd managed to capture a chair positioned to avoid direct eye contact. Because... touching his face? She definitely should not have done that. The light bristle of his stubble was branded on her fingertip.

She'd been half in love with the guy for ages, but that day in Ainsley's kitchen when he'd lifted her to the stool and gently picked the glass out of her heel had slammed the gate-of-no-return behind her. She was locked in a corral with her very awake feelings, and she didn't want to escape.

What she *did* want was for him to feel them, too... and then not shy away from expressing them. While she was dreaming, might as well go big.

"I thought all women were crazy about chocolate." Ryder leaned forward to see her around his stepmom.

So much for staying out of his line of vision. "I like the taste as much as the next girl. But it's not usually worth the reaction."

"Chocolate is high in histamines." Vivienne swirled some whipped cream on her fork and ate it before seeming to notice everyone was staring at her. "What? It's a proven scientific fact."

Alexia rolled her eyes. "You don't have to let your inner nerd out."

"I like my inner nerd, thank you very much. If I didn't, I wouldn't be planning to go to college for something medical."

That piqued Carey's attention. "Do you want to be a doctor?" And, if so, why hadn't the teen continued straight on after high school? Vivienne should get started.

"No, I don't think so. Takes too long and costs too much." Vivienne took a quick glance at Kathryn then bounced to her feet. "Anyone else done? I'll take plates back into the kitchen."

It cost too much? The girl's father was loaded, wasn't he? One look around Rockstead — not that Carey had visited the main ranch often — and you'd never think there was a problem with income. None of Vivienne's brothers had gone to college, but wasn't that more because they preferred ranch work? So, it probably came down to Declan not readily acknowledging that Vivienne was his daughter.

At least Carey's earlier suspicions that Vivienne might be

her own half-sister had been put to rest when they'd discovered Declan was Viv's father.

Carey handed over her plate and glanced at Ryder. He scowled as he stared off, his lip clamped against his teeth. What was he thinking?

Then, with a visible shake, the frown cleared, and his usual pleasant expression returned. He said something to Emma, who laughed.

Had Carey really seen that dark look, or was it all in her admittedly overactive imagination? It was so unlike anything she'd ever noticed with Ryder before. He always came across so casual and easygoing, almost placid, but in those unguarded seconds, there'd been something else visible.

She shivered just a little. That something had seemed feral, and she'd be lying if she pretended she didn't find it a wee bit sexy. Who knew Ryder Cavanagh had some Heathcliff lurking beneath the surface? Honestly, there wasn't much he could keep submerged there that would lessen his appeal.

Granny Wilson would totally flip if she could see into Carey's mind now. The word sexy would never have slipped past Granny's lips. Wouldn't even have found its way into Granny's puritan mind to start with, let alone released. She'd even been scandalized by some of the rakish heroes in those Georgette Heyer stories, the ones where dukes' hooded gazes lingered on ladies' ankles. Hadn't stopped her from reading the next one, though.

Imagine what one of those dukes would have thought while looking at his heroine's feet! Oh, the horror.

At least, Granny would have thought so.

"Have you girls finished your homework?" Aunt Kathryn turned to the twins.

Alexia threw her head back dramatically. "*Mom*. I have all weekend."

"Mine's done," Emma said primly.

Carey stifled a grin as she rose to her feet. "I should get going. Thanks again for the invitation."

"I'm so glad you came. I feel so badly that I don't know you better, my own niece."

"Life hasn't exactly been normal." Whatever normal was.

Vivienne poked her face out of the kitchen. "If you give me a minute, I'll copy out the recipe for you. It's old-school, like handwritten on one of those little cards."

"I have my granny's recipe box full of cards like that. There are some definite gems in there."

The younger woman's eyes brightened. "I'd love to peek at it sometime."

"Sure. There are no family secrets hidden in there."

In her periphery, Carey noticed Ryder flinch. What on earth? Why would that remark startle him? It was like he expected deep, dark mysteries to be buried in a recipe box. The thing wasn't a treasure chest full of hoarded gold and jewels.

She could only wish.

Carey followed Viv into the kitchen, glancing back at Ryder over her shoulder at the last second.

He was watching her, his expression totally blank. Did the cowboy have no emotions? There'd been one a bit ago, but they crossed his face so rarely that she wasn't practiced in reading them.

If she spent more time in his presence, it would help.

Except it wouldn't, because there was no future for them together. What had she been thinking, moving back to Jewel Lake? Laurel was right. Carey should have stayed in

Missoula. It wasn't that far to drive to hang out with Ainsley. She'd had a good job and could have found a nicer apartment.

But she'd had no idea how Ryder Cavanagh would capture her attention back then. If she'd guessed, she'd have stayed away.

RYDER CROSSED his boots then sat up straighter and crossed his arms instead. He would not look toward the kitchen. In fact, it would be a good idea to have left before Carey came back out with the recipe.

He glanced between the twins. "You're coming up to the ranch? I'm heading out."

"Don't be in such an all-fired panic, Ryder." Alexia grimaced. "We need to help clean up the kitchen and pack our stuff."

That was going to take longer than he wanted, but it wasn't like he had a choice. Ryder tapped his watch. "Time's a'wasting."

Emma surged to her feet. "You can clean the kitchen, Ry. That way we'll all be ready when Lex and I are packed."

"He probably doesn't know how to do that any more than he knows how to whip cream."

"Hey! Of course, I know how to clean a kitchen."

Smirking, Alexia jabbed both pointer fingers toward him in a gotcha motion. "We'll be back in ten."

Kathryn chuckled. "They're smooth."

"Aren't they, though?" But Ryder knew when he was beat. As much as he didn't want to catch another glimpse of Carey, there was also that part of him wanting to bask in her presence for the rest of his natural life. As though he liked living on the edge of a sharp blade.

He stood and stretched, not wanting to look too eager, then met Kathryn's gaze. "You doing okay?"

"Sure." Her smile was quick.

Too quick? And why would she confide in Ryder, anyway? "The girls say Dad's been coming to counseling with you."

Kathryn nodded. "It's true."

He couldn't resist. "And?"

"It's not steady progress, but it's progress. It's too early to know what kind of results to expect. I do value your prayers, Ryder."

In other words, pray... and shut up. "Okay." Kathryn had never been one to spill dirt about Dad. She'd maybe kept everything *too* close for too many years as she spiraled into depression. But now she was better... right? At least she was off the ranch, had a job, and had somehow convinced Dad to seek counseling.

Possibly more like coerced him. But he'd still had a choice.

There was always a choice.

Ryder had some, too. Stick his neck out there so Carey could reject him, and his brothers could laugh at his presumption... or not. Keep pursuing Jason Anderson... or not.

Suddenly, he could see how Kathryn had simply withdrawn bit by bit. Some decisions were hard, and it was much easier to put them off until another day. As long as he didn't push things to a head, there was always the chance of an accidentally excellent outcome. But if he pushed prematurely...

It didn't matter, anyway. Because with Carey, there'd be no difference if he made a move or not. The result would be the same. This way, at least, he could live in his imaginary world for a bit longer. Was that so bad?

Like now. Ryder sauntered across the space and into the kitchen. Vivienne perched on a tall stool by the counter, copying the recipe from one little card to another, while Carey ran hot water into the sink.

"Hey, you shouldn't have to clean up. You're a guest."

She flashed him a grin as she squirted dish soap. "I'm just getting things started while I wait."

Looked like she'd done more than start. All the little plates were stacked on the counter, and someone had wiped up the spatters of whipped cream where he'd gone a little crazy earlier.

Too bad Kathryn's apartment hadn't come with a dishwasher. No wonder the twins wanted to spend the weekend at Rockstead, where Cook wouldn't insist they help with either cooking or cleanup. It was probably good for them, though.

Ryder's gaze caught on a tea towel hanging from a hook. "I'll dry."

Carey's eyes widened. "Okay?"

"You sound skeptical. I know how."

"Hopefully, better than you know how to whip cream," muttered Vivienne.

"Of course." He snapped the tea towel at his younger sister then turned to Carey. "Ready whenever."

She set a stack of plates in the sudsy water and began washing then setting them in the drain rack, one at a time.

Ryder waited until her hands were buried in bubbles again before picking up each plate and wiping it dry. Not a chance did he want to accidentally brush her hand over that drain rack. Not when his cheek still tingled from when she'd wiped away the whipped cream earlier.

She'd flinched. Had it been so awful touching his stubble?

If he'd known she'd been invited for cake, he'd have shaved before coming to town. He'd have grabbed a shower and a clean shirt and worn his newer cowboy boots.

He'd probably have made a fool of himself.

Oh. He'd done that anyway. Also, it didn't matter if he made a good impression. Nothing was going to come of his little infatuation. He'd get over it — someday — and he'd laugh at how he'd let his emotions get tangled up in Carey Anderson. You know, when he'd fallen in love for real. Then he'd remember how silly this stage had been.

"Do the twins often come up for the weekend?"

Ryder blinked Carey's face into focus. "Sometimes. Sometimes just for a few hours here and there."

"Do you ever go, Vivienne?"

Right. There was someone else in the room, another reminder to watch his Ps and Qs.

"For the weekend? Ha. As if I want to hang around Declan."

"He's not there much, except at mealtime," Ryder said. Not that it would help.

"Which is too often. Not a chance. I'll go for a ride with the twins once in a while, but other than that? Nope. I made the first move, and look where that got me."

"I'm so sorry." Carey glanced over her shoulder at Vivienne as she slid a handful of forks into the drain rack basket. "I know what it's like to not have a relationship with a dad."

Ryder swallowed hard as he set the plate he'd been drying in the cupboard. "You don't see yours often, then?"

Carey scrunched her nose. "Not much, no. Not since he moved to Maine years ago."

Maine. That was as far as Branson had tracked Jason Anderson, too. "What's he doing out there?"

"I'm not sure. He has a little place on the shore, though."

Visions of a gilded colonial mansion sprang into Ryder's mind. How could the guy afford something like that? He picked up another plate, keeping his face impassive. He sure didn't want Carey to suspect any curiosity about her father. "Sounds nice. When's the last time you saw him?"

"Three or four years." She scrubbed at a plate that already looked clean. "There. That's the last one."

"Good timing." Vivienne tucked her pen into a jar on the counter. "Just got the recipe copied. I made a couple of notes I know my mom changed."

"Thanks so much." Carey pulled the plug and wiped the sink as the water swirled away. "I should be going."

Ryder stood, paralyzed, as she picked up the card and waved goodbye without making further eye contact. Had he made her uncomfortable, or had there been something else going on?

He'd asked his brothers not to talk about the investigation he and Branson were involved in. Yes, thinking specifically of Ainsley's friendship with Carey. Not that he had anything to hide. Not like Jason Anderson seemed to, that was for sure. But he didn't know whether Carey was still close to her dad. If she'd tip him off. Now he was pretty sure those fears were unfounded, but still… the whole situation made him uncomfortable.

From the other room, he heard Kathryn's quiet voice saying good night to Carey. Heard the door close behind her.

He could breathe again.

Never mind the odd look Vivienne cast his way.

CHAPTER FIVE

W ait a minute." Ainsley narrowed her eyes and pointed her finger at Carey. "Are they trying to set you up with *Ryder*?"

Carey laughed. Hopefully it sounded like she thought her friend's words were a joke, because weren't they? "Are you kidding me? Don't forget Kathryn is my aunt. She only invited me because the girls needed to borrow sugar to make their cake."

"That's exactly what I mean. Kathryn has never run out of anything in her life. There isn't a chance in a million she didn't have a cup of sugar in the apartment."

"Maybe the girls had been on a baking binge, and she hadn't realized they were low?"

Ainsley scoffed.

Carey could see her friend's point, but what she *didn't* need was Ainsley catching wind of Carey's silly infatuation with the youngest Cavanagh brother. "Anyway, the cake was amazing, and Vivienne gave me your mom's recipe. I can't believe you never made it for me. You know how I react to chocolate."

"Sorry, I never thought of it. It was always Mom's and Viv's thing. I mean, it's okay, but I don't love molasses that much. It's not one of the four food groups."

"I don't even want to know where your brain went with that."

"You know, the four food groups are coffee, tacos, cheese, and chocolate."

"Why, again, are we friends?"

Ainsley chuckled. "Because you love me. But you can't put tea and molasses in place of coffee and chocolate as food groups. It's just wrong. Plus, no one would agree with you."

"Says you. Anyway, when I make your mom's recipe, I won't invite you over. I'll make cupcakes and eat them all myself."

"There goes your girlish figure."

"Fine. I'll freeze them and eat one a day. By myself."

"Maybe Ryder would join you."

"Your mind is just as warped over that as it is about the whole chocolate thing." Carey took a playful swing at her friend's head.

Ainsley ducked, laughing. "Aw, Ryder's not so bad. Kind of sweet, really."

"He's nice enough." Carey kept her voice even. "But a little young for me, don't you think? Besides, I'm not looking."

"Age doesn't make that big a difference once both parties are adults. It's only weird in high school."

"Easy for you to say. Nathaniel's two years older than you."

Ainsley shrugged. "I didn't know that when we first met. When he asked me out, I didn't say, wait, are you older than me?"

"Would you have dated him if you already knew he was several years younger?"

Ainsley's eyebrows shot up.

"Hypothetically, of course."

"You like him."

Carey furrowed her brow. "Like who? Nathaniel? Don't be silly — he's all yours."

"Nice attempt at deflection."

"I don't know what you're talking about."

"Let me clarify so there's no doubt. You, Carey Anderson, have a thing for Ryder Cavanagh."

Carey opened her mouth. Closed it. Her brain found no words fit for utterance.

"She *what?*"

At the sound of Nathaniel's voice, heat flashed up Carey's face, quicker than any chocolate-induced rosacea could hit her system.

Nathaniel stood in the doorway with Oakley in his arms, his eyebrows drawn together in disbelief. "What did I just walk in on?"

"A confessional." Ainsley eyed Carey. "One I think you'd best forget you overheard."

"I'm pretty sure what I heard. Is that true, Carey?"

"I… he's a nice guy. That's all."

A grin twitched around Nathaniel's lips. "This is rich."

"Nathaniel." Ainsley jumped to her feet and plucked their infant daughter from his grasp. "Promise me you won't say a thing. You weren't supposed to be home for another half hour at least. This wasn't for your ears."

The cowboy leaned down and pecked his wife's lips. "How are you going to bribe me to keep quiet? Hmm?"

Ainsley laid Oakley on the nearby sofa, wrapped both arms around him, and kissed him thoroughly.

Carey didn't want to watch. Blushing, she scooped the

baby into her arms. "Come to Auntie Carey, Oakley. Don't watch your mama and papa make out."

"Young as she is, she's seen worse." Nathaniel laughed and went silent again.

Carey dared a quick glance before turning her back completely. Never mind the infant. This was way more than *she* needed to see, either.

"You almost have me convinced, wife," Nathaniel murmured.

Enough. Carey opened the French door to the patio and stepped outside, barely stopping herself from fanning her face. Yikes. She'd never meant to slip up at all. Never meant to let Ainsley guess, let alone Nathaniel. And that all came after Vivienne's raised eyebrows last night. And the suspicious invitation for cake when Ryder was also present.

There was only one thing for it. She needed to back away from all the Cavanaghs for a while, including Ainsley. She'd stay busy with work. She'd volunteer at church. Maybe she'd join the Pot of Gold Treasure Hunt this summer. The coordinator might be able to use help in the office. And hadn't Pastor Marshall Smith asked for volunteers for the youth group during yesterday's service?

Alexia and Emma attended youth, so Carey should find a different place to serve. Although, while Ryder might be younger than she was, he'd definitely outgrown that group. Maybe it would be okay.

Or she could stop by the church office and talk to Mrs. McDiarmid. The receptionist would know where the openings were. Eli Bryson, the youth pastor, was dating Stephanie Simpson, so Mrs. McDiarmid wouldn't suspect Carey of being after him. But the woman was super gossipy, so... maybe not the church at all.

Carey would think of something.

The door opened behind her. "Safe to come in now," Ainsley said with a laugh.

"Are you sure?"

"Yeah. Nathaniel will keep what I said to himself. It helps that you didn't admit anything." Ainsley leaned on the railing beside Carey and glanced over. "But he's gone again now, so if you want to continue this conversation, he won't overhear your confession."

"I do not, in fact, wish to continue this conversation." Carey kept her voice stiff.

Ainsley nudged her with her elbow. "Aw, come on. Didn't I tell you everything?"

"You did not. I was away at college when you first met Nathaniel, and you didn't tell me his name, just that you'd met someone amazing. That hardly qualifies as *everything*."

"You're right. I wish I could remember why I didn't tell you. Maybe because I knew you were his cousin?"

How could Carey stay angry with Ainsley after everything her friend had endured? Ainsley's mom, Brenda, didn't even know or care who her father was, just that he was some guy she'd met at a party in college. Then Brenda had worked for Carey's dad and left in a hurry when she'd become pregnant with Declan Cavanagh's daughter, Vivienne. Later, Brenda had been furious when Ainsley returned to Jewel Lake and fell in love with Nathaniel, and when Ainsley had suffered a traumatic brain injury, her mother had used that to her advantage to keep the lovers apart, even though Ainsley was pregnant with Bella.

Ainsley had suffered a far worse childhood than Carey had. After the divorce, Mom had moved in with Granny in Missoula for a couple of years. Dad had eventually sent a decent settlement after he shut down his insurance business and moved to Maine.

Carey hugged Ainsley and transferred the baby girl to her mother. "It's okay. Whatever happened back then doesn't matter anymore. Our friendship survived it all, and we're good now. I shouldn't have brought it up."

"We're quite a pair. Maybe that's why we're friends. We understand what it's like growing up in a dysfunctional household. I can't even call mine a family, not really."

"Your mom loved you."

Ainsley scoffed. "She had some strange ways of showing it." She cradled her infant in her arms and pressed kisses to her face. "When I think how much love I have for this child... I'd do anything for her and Bella. I'd live in a hut in the forest and subsist on air if that would make their lives better. I just don't understand why my mom didn't love me that much."

"I have no answer." At least Carey's mom had kept her daughters together and done what she could after the divorce. She hadn't even dated again for nearly a decade, until Laurel and Carey were in high school.

And then there was Monica Cavanagh. It was a wonder Ryder had turned out so well with Declan for a father and a mother who'd abandoned her three sons.

But that was not a direction Carey was willing to turn the conversation. Not now. Probably not ever.

IT HADN'T ESCAPED Ryder's notice that he'd become the stablehand again over the winter. It had been a lovely respite last year to have Taryn in charge of mucking out stalls and exercising horses and keeping the tack organized for the few months she'd been at Rockstead. Then, over the winter, everyone pitched in.

But he wasn't going to clean up behind the twins. "Hey, Lex. Domino's bridle belongs on its hook."

Alexia rolled her eyes. "It's fine where it is."

"It's not fine. You know better."

"Ry..."

"Don't bother. You know the rules around here."

She leaned closer. "I don't live here."

"You're definitely not a guest. Clean up or—"

"Or you'll tell Dad?"

Alexia had him there. He definitely wouldn't be wandering off tattling on the girls.

"Tell me what?" Dad's voice came from behind him.

Now *that* was timing. It wasn't the first time Ryder had noticed Dad skulking around the stables, but it wasn't usually quite this convenient. Ryder cocked his eyebrow at his younger sister.

"Nothing, Daddy," she called sweetly, completely at odds with the ugly scowl she directed at Ryder. "We're just joking around."

"Doesn't look like nothing."

Alexia's expression schooled instantly as she looked past Ryder's shoulder.

He smirked at her then crossed his arms and turned to take in their father standing in the tack room doorway.

"Daddy, do you need to hire a new stablehand? Ryder isn't doing that great a job."

Dad's eyes flicked to Ryder then narrowed on Alexia. "Got someone in mind?"

"There's this boy at school who needs a part-time job."

"No."

"You don't even know who I mean. He's—"

"Doesn't matter. I'm not hiring some snot-nosed kid for you to flirt with."

"But..."

Dad's gaze hardened, and his glower deepened.

Ryder found his mouth moving. "Vivienne might like to work here."

"Still no." Dad's eyes all but pierced Ryder's skin before shifting back to Lex. "We're doing just fine on our own around here, so long as everyone cleans up behind themselves. That includes you putting your tack *exactly* back where it belongs, Alexia, and scrubbing out Domino's stall when you're here." He looked pointedly at the bridle draped askew over the saddle.

Alexia sighed and hung it from its hook with dramatic flair. "Are you happy now?"

"No."

"Well, it's not my fault you're grouchy all the time."

Oh, boy. Living in town with her mother had not taught this sixteen-year-old any wisdom or tact. Ryder eyed the distance to the door, but his father seemed to have grown several inches and widened forty pounds as he drew himself up. There was no getting around Dad unless he allowed it. And Ryder would rather not draw attention to himself.

"Is there anything else you'd like to say while your mouth is running off like a spring colt?" Dad's voice sounded like he'd laced it with ice cubes.

"Yeah." Alexia straightened and looked Dad in the eye. "There is. How come you hate me and Emma so much?"

Ryder's gaze shifted to Dad who just stared at his daughter.

"Don't try to deny it. All our friends have dads who take

them riding and on vacations and to concerts and rodeos. Or they help with homework or play games or stuff. You never do a single thing with me and Em except growl and snarl."

Dad's jaw tensed, and he blinked a couple of times.

Emotion? Couldn't be. Not Declan Cavanagh.

"And don't even get me started on Vivienne. I bet she wishes she'd never even heard of you. You are absolutely horrid to her."

"Anything else?"

Alexia burst into tears and rushed past Dad, who stepped aside and watched her go. Her boots clattered on the tiled alleyway then Domino's gate squeaked open.

Ryder should take a can of WD-40 to the hinge later. But... right now... what would Dad say or do if he went after Alexia? Or simply walked away at all.

"I've wondered when that was coming." Dad looked at Ryder. "So, while we're here, do you have anything you'd like to add?"

"No, sir."

"Oh, really?" One eyebrow peaked. "I'm sure my sons are just as fond of me as my daughters are. Just not hormonal enough to dump it all out."

"Why are you goading me?" The words left Ryder of their own free will. "You have my respect. Sir."

"I suppose you want *love*, too. Like your sisters. Like their mother."

"I think everyone wants love." Ryder cleared his throat. "Sir."

"How does anyone get anything done if it's all mushy this and lovey-dovey that?"

"Maybe they get less done, but they're happier. Or maybe

49

it's more fun to work together with someone they love as a partner."

"Don't tell me you've fallen for that whole sappy nonsense, too. Who's the girl?"

"No, sir." Not a chance was Ryder opening the crack to let Declan see inside. He'd already said way too much for a guy who ate most meals with only his sullen father for company.

Dad grunted and pivoted away.

Should Ryder go after him? Try to make him see how he drove everyone away? No. Alexia needed him more.

CHAPTER SIX

I t had been a week since Ainsley had discovered Carey's secret, or thought she had. That Sunday, Carey had gone to church in Missoula and out for lunch with her sister.

Perfectly acceptable.

She'd been busy every evening with all kinds of made-up things.

On Saturday morning, she heard about a group of twenty-somethings from the church who were planning a hike up Miner's Bluff. Carey hesitated, then decided to go. Odds of any of the Cavanagh brothers or their wives joining in were slim to none.

In the parking lot around the other side of the lake, she took a swig of her water bottle before tucking it in her day pack's side pocket.

"Hey, Carey! It's good to see you."

Carey smiled at Stephanie Simpson. "Hi! It looks like a great day for a hike."

The May sun shone brightly across Jewel Lake and illuminated the newly leafed aspens.

Stephanie bounced a little on her heels and glanced around the group. "Sure is!"

"I haven't been up to the top since I was a kid. Maybe you know how it is, always too busy to do the local stuff."

"Eli loves to hike." Stephanie giggled as she glanced at her boyfriend. "I've spent more time in nature since we started dating than the rest of my life put together."

Would it be that way if Carey and Ryder got together? She hadn't done much riding, and that was practically Ryder's life. He probably loved all sorts of outdoors pursuits.

"I'm so excited to get to know you better." Stephanie's smile turned back to Carey.

"Looks like most of the group are couples."

"Yeah. That's Dale and Trinity over there. He owns Communication Location downtown, and she's a potter. Dale's brother and his wife used to hike with us a lot, but they just had a set of twins a couple of months ago. I can't imagine."

Aunt Kathryn had given birth to two sets, albeit thirteen years apart.

"And that's Caleb, Trinity's brother. He and Sage — she works at town hall — are newlyweds."

"What does Caleb do?"

Stephanie waved her hand. "He's some sort of tech genius who works remotely. I think."

"Everyone ready? Let's hit the trail!" Eli gestured toward the dirt path headed into the trees along the shoreline.

The group fell into a single line with Caleb at the lead. Carey hiked behind Stephanie who hiked behind Eli. That couple might be dating, but from Carey's observation,

Stephanie was far more into the youth pastor than he was into her. When the trail widened a little, Stephanie skipped to catch up to Eli and twine her fingers through his.

Okay, fine. Carey had suspected she'd be the odd one out, so it shouldn't surprise her.

Eli glanced over his shoulder and offered her a warm smile. "Hey, Carey. Good to see you today. Ever hiked up here before?"

"Not since I was a kid."

"Well, welcome back. It's one of my favorite quick hikes."

"Mine, too." Stephanie beamed up at him.

Note to self: don't be so stinking obvious when you like a guy, even if he says he likes you back. Ainsley hadn't been nearly this sappy, nor had Dafne or Taryn before they'd married Blake and Noah.

It was educational watching this pair, but Eli was a big boy. He could take care of himself.

"The view is so amazing from up top, isn't it, Eli?" Stephanie squeezed his hand.

He flashed her a grin. "It really is." He looked up the trail "Hey, Trinity! Let me get that for you." Eli jogged past the others and helped Trinity with her water bottle.

Not that she needed help, most likely. Her husband wasn't far away, just yakking with Caleb. Maybe Eli was trying to get away from Stephanie.

That couldn't be, though. They were dating. He wouldn't ask a woman out if he didn't like her, would he?

Maybe Carey was just as noticeable in her fixation on Ryder Cavanagh. Ainsley had caught on. Maybe Ryder had, too, and was just as intent as Eli Bryson in finding a way to ease away without hurting her feelings. Because if Ryder shared them, wouldn't he let her know?

He kind of had. Right? The way he kept looking at her.

Maybe he'd been looking at her so he'd know where she was and could shift elsewhere, like Eli seemed to be doing right now.

Carey hadn't wondered so much what a guy thought of her since high school. This was ridiculous. Maybe she should put herself forward and see what happened. It couldn't be worse than wondering for the next five years.

But maybe Ryder was like Eli, too polite to actually tell a woman he wasn't interested, or wasn't interested *anymore*. And maybe Carey was too steeped in Regency England to make the first move, anyway. Although some of those heroines—

She nearly slammed into Dale's back when he came to a halt on the trail in front of her. "Oh! Sorry."

He grinned at her over his shoulder. "Just stopping at the pictographs for a minute so Caleb and Sage can argue about what some of those prehistoric paintings actually represent. Not that anyone knows for sure, not even the local native tribes."

Stephanie sidled past Dale and Trinity, and — surprise — stopped beside Eli as she grappled for her water bottle in her pack's side pocket. "Oops. Can't quite get it." She smiled up at Eli. "Would you mind?"

He tugged out the bottle and handed it to her with a fleeting grin. "Here you go."

Dale chuckled.

Carey looked at him, eyebrows raised. "What's so funny?"

"Nothing."

His wife twined her fingers through his. "It's Stephanie. She's been chasing Eli forever, and now that she's caught him, she's not sure what to do with him."

To Carey's eye, it was more that Eli wasn't sure. That pair was headed for a breakup as surely as she'd get rosacea from eating the next brownie. But it wasn't polite to speculate. "I heard Mrs. McDiarmid had a heart attack. Is she going to be okay?" Maybe that was still gossip. Whatever.

"She'll probably be in the hospital for a few more days, but it will be weeks before she'll be back in the church office."

"Oh, no! How will Pastor Marshall and Eli manage without her?" Carey glanced toward the others. Maybe it was a good thing Stephanie worked full-time at the bank, or she'd be right there in Eli's face all week long.

"Harper Satterfield is stepping in, I think. She's here for the summer to oversee the marina project for her father's company but said she could split her time easily."

"Oh, that's convenient. I heard about the investment company coming in, so that's great."

Trinity nodded. "Yes, it should work out well. Hopefully Mrs. McDiarmid will be ready to get back in the office before too long. I'm sure she won't be satisfied with how anyone else will do things."

"I believe it." Carey chuckled. "Good help is hard to find, especially when someone has been doing the same job for as long as she has. Mrs. McDiarmid ran that church office when I was a kid."

"I know, right? I remember that, too." Trinity smiled. "I'm sorry we didn't know each other well back then, but I guess we all had our things going on."

Had they ever. Trinity and Caleb's parents' split had been just as dramatic as hers. Carey had heard about it clear in Missoula when she was in high school.

It was good to be back in Jewel Lake, getting reacquainted with people she'd known in her childhood. This group was sort of like the Cavanagh brothers, though less threatening since Ryder wasn't part of it. But this crew was all paired off, too, even if Eli and Stephanie seemed shaky. Eli might be a nice enough guy, but he wasn't Ryder.

So much for keeping Ryder out of her head.

RYDER HADN'T SEEN Carey in a couple of weeks, and there wasn't anyone he could ask if she was okay. And that was how he found himself pressing the buzzer for Kathryn's apartment on a Friday evening while ignoring the other button marked C. Anderson.

Carey's car was in the lot, but he had no real reason to contact her. He could just hear the conversation.

Hi, it's Ryder. Can I come up?

And then she'd laugh and ask what on earth for. Of course, she would.

But… what if she didn't laugh? At least then he'd know. Either way, he'd know.

Vivienne's voice came through the intercom. "Is that you, Ry?"

"Yes, can I come up?"

"Sure. I saw your truck in the lot." Bzzzt.

He passed Carey's floor and emerged on the third level. His half-sister poked her head into the corridor as he neared. Ryder grinned at her. "Hey, thanks. Is Kathryn home?"

Vivienne shook her head. "She has a staff meeting this evening."

"On a Friday?"

"Yeah. I know it's weird, but it has to do with graduation ceremonies in a couple of weeks."

They didn't have a Cavanagh graduate this year. Last year it had been Viv. Next year it would be the twins. Wow, wasn't that hard to believe? Ryder stood in the corridor, feeling awkward with his sister. He should have put more effort into getting to know her. Instead, he'd left it mostly up to the girls.

"Come on in, and I'll make a pot of tea. It's just me, though. The twins are at youth."

"Um, okay." He really should have called ahead.

"I made some salted caramel cookies."

"Sounds good." Ryder followed her in and closed the door behind himself. "Can I give you a hand?"

"Nah, I'll just be a minute."

He took off his cowboy hat, hung it on a hook, and ran his fingers through his flattened hair. Near the hat rack was a large, framed photo taken at Blake and Dafne's wedding last summer. Dad, looking uncomfortable, stood clear at one end beside Travis, while Kathryn stood close to the other end between Noah and Nathaniel.

Ryder hadn't seen this photo before. Hadn't seen more than a few snapshots from the wedding, though he'd noticed his sisters-in-law gathered around albums on occasion.

This, though. He catalogued everyone. The three teen girls beside the newlyweds. Travis, Nathaniel, Adam, and their families gathered around. Noah and Ryder awkwardly single.

Hadn't lasted much longer for Noah. He and Taryn, who wasn't even in the photo, had eloped just a few weeks later.

"Kathryn finally got the enlargements last week," came Viv's voice from beside him.

"There are a lot of us." Nothing like speaking the obvious, cowboy.

His sister laughed. "True that. I never dreamed, growing

up, that I had a family this big. It was just Mom, Ainsley, and me for seventeen years."

He angled a look at her. "We must have come as quite a shock."

She sighed. "Yeah."

"I'd apologize for our father if I thought it would help."

"It's him being a jerk, not you. Not any of you. I don't feel like I belong, but it is what it is."

Ryder slung his arm across her shoulders. "I'm sorry. I don't know if any of us feels like we belong. Not really. We've got such a mishmash of parents and steps and halfs and... it's a confusing mess."

"But at least you always knew who your parents were."

He harrumphed. "I barely remember when my mom left. Travis and Blake have more memories, mostly of our parents fighting."

"I'm sorry. That doesn't sound great." Vivienne studied him. "Why is he so horrible?"

She deserved a real answer, more than 'that's just how he is.' While Ryder mulled, the kettle whistled, and Vivienne turned back into the kitchen to make tea.

He followed, leaning against the doorway. "All I know is he's been fighting God in a big way."

Vivienne plated cookies. "That doesn't make everyone into blockheads."

"No, you're right, but it's the best I've got. There for a bit when the twins were babies, I thought we had a pretty good family. Everyone got along except Travis and Adam. Dad and Kathryn seemed happy."

"While he was hiding that he knew I existed." Vivienne plunked the carton of cream on the table so hard that some sloshed out.

"I guess so." Did that make *all* of Ryder's memories suspect? Why couldn't that brief happiness have come without such a cost? "Look, I get that it must've been hard not to know your history, and to know your father didn't want you."

"Still doesn't want me."

Ryder tipped his head in acknowledgment. "I mean, I get it, but at least your mom protected you from being raised by Declan. My mother abandoned my brothers and me to him."

Her shoulders slumped. "I guess."

"Why are you sticking around, Viv?" He hesitated, but this was a question he'd wondered for the entire past year and a half. "If this is all too hard, why stay?"

She swiped moisture from her eyes.

Ryder's heart constricted. "I'm sorry. I shouldn't have asked you that. I, for one, am glad you're here."

"Where else can I go? My mom's gone. All I have is my sister, and she's one of *you* now. I may have been raised with Ainsley, but you are just as much my sibling as she is. Half-belonging everywhere means I belong nowhere."

At least Ryder had always felt grounded at the ranch. Monica might have left. Declan might be cold and sullen. Kathryn might have slowly withdrawn. Rockstead Ranch had always been the one constant. Like his brothers, he couldn't imagine living or working anywhere else.

Blake's jab that Ryder might need to leave the ranch once in a while if he wanted to meet a girl surfaced, but he shoved it back under.

"Come up to the ranch tomorrow. Come riding with me."

"I have to work. I'm finally getting more hours."

"I thought you were going to quit at From Stetsons to Spurs."

"I'd love to, but I haven't been able to find a better job. I need to save money for college."

"Have you asked Dad to pay your tuition?"

Vivienne stared at him from wide eyes. "You are kidding me, right? He hasn't said five civil words to me in all these months. I'm certainly not going to lead with that."

Ryder's mind scrambled in five directions at once. When the smoke cleared, he had a plan. "We need a stablehand. Would you like to give it a try?"

"You have absolutely lost your marbles."

He shook his head. "I'm pretty sure this will work. Come up Sunday after church and let me show you what the job would entail. If Riley could do it — and Taryn — I bet you could, too. Dad didn't have to like either of their presence, but then, neither of them were his daughters."

"You're crazy. He's the one in charge, not you. There is no way he'd welcome me up there and put me on payroll."

"I'm not so sure." Ryder reached for a cookie and ate it in three bites. "Let me work this angle and see what happens. You in?"

"No."

"Look, the guys will be on our side as soon as they hear. This will work. You know what they say. If you want a different result, you have to do something different. Same old methods get you the same old results."

"Ry. I'm not sure."

"Trust me. Let's give this a shot."

And then... could he man up and take his own advice? Because his same old indecision about Carey was only getting him the same old results: a woman who didn't even know she was constantly on his mind.

CHAPTER SEVEN

Carey felt Ainsley's elbow digging into her side. Uh oh. What had her friend caught this time?

"Don't even try to deny you were watching Ryder," Ainsley whispered.

Okay. Still, deflection. "He looks like a man on a mission. That's what caught my attention. Don't he and Vivienne usually go to lunch with you guys at the Golden Grill?"

The siblings had just left the church building together, a mere three seconds after Pastor Smith's benediction. If that.

"Usually. As you know." Ainsley grinned.

"I'll go get Bella from nursery." Nathaniel settled Oakley into Ainsley's arms and pressed a kiss to the top of her head before looking at Carey. "Coming for lunch with the gang?"

It didn't look like Ryder would be there, although he and his sister might only have a quick errand to do first. Besides, hadn't Carey decided to get brave and make the first move? Not in front of all his brothers, though. "Sure. Sounds good."

"Back in five." Nathaniel wended his way through the crowd leaving the sanctuary.

"You need to spill, girl." Ainsley nudged her again.

Carey tried for a casual laugh. Probably failed. "You've made up your mind, huh?"

"You are such a bad liar and even worse at side-stepping. The more I've been thinking about it, the more I can totally see it. I'm pretty sure it's mutual."

Carey's heart jolted. "You think so?"

"Gotcha."

"Don't even." She took a step back.

"Aw, it's okay. Really, it is. But you might need a little help getting through to him."

"No. Don't you dare."

Ainsley tapped her chin. "This is way too much fun. I didn't get to help Blake or Noah snag their brides, so I think I'm due."

Carey shook her head and backed up another step.

"Don't you trust me?"

"Not even this much." She smashed her fingertip tight against her thumb.

"Well, I happen to believe I'm perfectly trustworthy. Come for lunch at the Grill — I have it on good authority Ryder will not be present — and then come up to the house afterward. You've been avoiding me for a couple of weeks. Don't think I didn't notice. But you're coming today. I've already got elk stew in the slow cooker." Ainsley leaned closer. "Oakley is due some time with her Auntie Carey."

It was kind of hard to argue with Ainsley when she got this way.

RYDER FELT like he'd swallowed a live octopus, and all eight tentacles were writhing to their own tempos, trying to escape the confines of his belly.

He'd run his idea past his brothers, and they all thought he'd lost his marbles, at best. Finally, Travis had slapped him on the back hard enough to rattle his molars and said, "It's your skin, Ry. It's been nice knowing you."

Across the truck cab, Vivienne stared out the windshield, so immobile Ryder could see no sign of life.

Did he have a death wish?

He absolutely did not, but it might be hard to prove at the moment. *Last chance to turn around.* If he said that out loud, odds were about 100 to zero his kid sister would take him up on it.

God? But his mind wouldn't settle enough for a coherent prayer. He'd been praying since Friday evening, and the sense this needed doing had not left him. That didn't keep him from shaking in his boots.

Ryder rounded the last curve and parked his pickup beside the corral. Several horses, his own Champlain in the midst, flicked their tails at early-season flies. Sam, one of the ranch collies, wandered out of the stable as he stretched, then came toward the truck wagging his plume.

It was hard to imagine a more peaceful place.

Illusion.

Ryder glanced across the cab. "Ready?"

Vivienne's head shook quickly. "Not even a little bit."

"You'll be fine. I'll be right beside you." Movement in his truck's side-mount mirror caught his attention. His father — Viv's father — strode across from the house. "Show time."

His sister's chin came up. "Already?"

"Yup. He's on his way."

Vivienne pushed open the truck door and dropped out.

Ryder did the same and rounded the vehicle, so he was between his sister and his father. "Hey, Dad."

Declan jerked to a stop, his dark eyes swinging between the two of them before his eyebrows peaked. "Going for a ride?"

Ryder nodded. "We're planning to, yes. First, I'd like to show Vivienne around more."

"She's been here before."

"Right. But you need a stablehand, and she needs a job and a place to stay. I happen to know we've got four vacant cabins."

Dad's eyes narrowed. "No."

"You hired Riley on Adam's say-so. You hired Taryn on Nathaniel's. So, please hire your own daughter for the sake of the entire family."

"She doesn't know her way around horses."

Whose fault was that? Ryder bit back the question. "Riley had only been on a horse a handful of times. She learned fast. Taryn had ridden but she'd never cared for her mount. Hadn't even saddled up on her own. She learned, too. I think you'll find Viv's a quick study. She's a Cavanagh, after all. Horses are in her blood."

Vivienne inhaled sharply, and Dad's scowl deepened.

"At least you know she's not here because I have a crush on her. She's my sister. I'll help her get her feet under her. Teach her everything she needs to know."

"You don't know what you're asking."

"I think I do. You're trying to hold onto the status quo, but you know what? It's gone. You can't even find it in the rear-view mirror anymore. Kathryn's gone. The twins are gone.

You have the tools to get them back. You just need to use them."

"Anything else?" Dad ground the words out between clenched teeth.

"Give Vivienne a chance. The rest of us have accepted her into the family. It's just you pretending she doesn't exist. You know what, Dad? She exists. She's your daughter. Give her a job. Get to know her. Embrace life the way it is now, and you can help shape the future of Rockstead Ranch and the Cavanagh clan."

Declan didn't move a single muscle, but Ryder felt his piercing gaze through to the bone.

Ryder took a deep breath. "God's waiting for you to realize He's the King of the universe, not you. Not saying it's easy to let go of the reins and trust Him, but it's worth it."

"What do you know? You're still wet behind the ears."

"I'm almost twenty-five. There's plenty of control freak in me." And some of it manifested in how he pulled back when he couldn't be certain of a positive outcome. Well, that ended today. Had already ended, regardless of Dad's final word on this topic.

Dad shifted his gaze from Ryder to Vivienne. It was the first time he'd looked straight at her, as far as Ryder knew.

Viv lifted her chin and stared straight back.

Atta girl, sis. Show that Cavanagh backbone. We weren't made to be walked all over.

"One week." Declan pivoted and strode away.

"No." Vivienne's voice rang clear.

He swung back. "What do you mean, no? Ryder did all that groveling for nothing, just so you could turn down a probationary position?" He glared between them. "You were just making a point?"

"I have a job now. I hate it, but I haven't been there long enough to earn vacation time. If I quit that job, I need more of a guarantee that you're not playing around with me."

Ryder slung his arm across his sister's shoulders. "A trial period is common."

"For *family*?" She twisted away from him and stomped closer to their father. "I know you sent money to my mom all those years, but you know what? That didn't make up for the childhood I had. The insecurity. The not-knowing."

"She did what she thought was best."

"You probably threatened her."

Oh, boy. Don't push all the Declan buttons at once.

Dad's eyebrows shot up beneath his Stetson. "You're being overly dramatic. If you're going to work for me, you'll learn to keep your emotions out of it."

"The kids you love and acknowledge always had a job with you. They had a place to live. They probably would have had their college paid for if they wanted it."

Declan crossed his arms and widened his stance.

"And that's what I want. I want to work here until college starts in fall. Then I want you to pick up the tab for nursing school. And I'd like to work here summers in between."

"Anything else?"

Ryder felt like he was watching a tennis match, the way the volleys flew back and forth. But once Viv got going, she was playing for keeps. He had to hand it to her. By his apparent capitulation, so did Dad.

"Treat me like one of the family." She raised a hand. "But, for the record, how you treat your entire family needs to change, because you're a bully."

"You know nothing," Dad snarled.

"Do we have a deal?"

"You have a *job*. You'd better learn it quickly. We'll talk about college later. And keep your opinions to yourself about how I run this family and this business."

Vivienne stuck her hand out. "Deal."

Declan did not shake it. He pivoted and stalked away.

Ryder allowed himself to breathe as he turned to his sister. "Welcome. I think."

DID Carey really want to be part of this wild, noisy family? Now she could see why Ainsley had wanted an open floor plan with plenty of space. The brothers — minus Ryder — had the Seahawks game on full blast at the other end of the great room while their wives clustered around the kitchen table. Dafne explained the rules to *Hand and Foot*, while Riley bounced Joseph and Dakota nursed Penelope.

Gavin and Toby had a toy ranch spread out beside the window overlooking the deck. Bella kept making off with chunky wooden horses, much to Toby's dismay. Technically, the entire set was Bella's, and the bigger boys would need to get over it.

Where were Ryder and Vivienne? No one commented on their absence or seemed to notice it. Well, Carey certainly wouldn't be the one to ask. Not after Ainsley's perceptive words after church. There was no point in making an announcement to the rest of the clan: *I'm only here because I have this insanely stupid crush on your kid brother.*

Yeah, no. It wasn't even true. Ryder wasn't the only reason. Carey had been friends with Ainsley since they were little. She'd gotten to know the other Cavanagh wives since her move back to Jewel Lake.

The other women she'd met at church and around town were great, too, but no one could compete with the bond she had with Ainsley. Besides, it was awkward hanging around that group, watching Stephanie cling to Eli. They were together, but Eli's head clearly wasn't in the game, and Carey didn't want to be the one to explain the situation to Stephanie.

There was no point in poking a stick into the spokes of Stephanie's dreams when it would lead nowhere but to a strained friendship. Not when Carey's own feelings for Ryder refused to go away.

Would her closeness with Ainsley be affected if Carey tried for a relationship with Ryder and it didn't work out? Ugh. She didn't want to think about that. But, surely not. She and Ainsley went way back.

A truck engine grew louder then cut out.

Carey's heart leaped. That would be Ryder. It had to be. He was the only one missing. Well, him and Vivienne, but they'd last been seen together, so they likely still were.

Why had she sat with her back to the door? Because it had been the last seat left at the table when she'd returned from the restroom. Now her senses all tuned in to the boot-steps crossing the deck and the door opening.

Someone muted the Seahawks game.

"Well?" Travis demanded.

"He said yes."

Whoops and cheers exploded from the other end of the great room.

Ryder's words had been clear, but the meaning? Not so much. A quick glance around the table revealed that Riley and Taryn looked as confused as Carey felt. But, at least, Ainsley turned in her chair, which freed Carey to do the same.

Ryder looked jubilant. There was no other word for it. But apprehension covered Vivienne's face.

Ainsley jumped to her feet. "That's great, right, sis?"

Vivienne shook her head, more in bemusement than denial. "I hope so. I feel like old Daniel tossed into the lion's den."

"God protected Daniel." Ainsley gave her sister a hug. "You'll do great."

"Would someone mind...?" Riley put in.

Ryder's gaze snagged on Carey's for a long moment before he lifted Vivienne's hand high. "You're looking at the newest stablehand for Rockstead Ranch. Viv is moving into Cabin Two next weekend — she needs to give her notice at the western wear shop before she can start full-time."

"Cabin Two! My old stomping grounds." Riley grinned.

"Mine, too." Taryn laughed. "Good for you. I hope it all works out."

Ryder draped his arm across Vivienne's shoulders. "Of course, Dad said no at first, but then I explained a few things to him, and then Viv did, and he relented."

"That's so awesome. I didn't give you a ghost of a chance of getting through to him." Blake shook his head. "Never discount the charm of the baby of the family."

"Which I'm not," Ryder said with a laugh. "You forgot for a minute we have three little sisters."

"Nah. Dafne's explained birth order to me. Somehow, it's all very important." Blake winked at his wife. "And you were the baby of both our initial family *and* the baby of our merged family until you were seven. That was plenty long enough to lock in your last-born personality. Get Daf to explain it all if you don't believe me."

"Whatever. The point is, Vivienne and I teamed up, tackled

Dad, and won. He's also considering paying for her college next year. So, I think God's working on him."

"Whoa. Nursing school, too?" Ainsley squealed. "I'm so happy for you, Viv!"

The family crowded around their sister, but Carey hung back. She wasn't family, after all.

Ryder's gaze found hers as he stepped aside from the melee himself.

Carey didn't let herself look away or pretend she hadn't noticed. She held his gaze for a few long seconds. Would he get the message she was attempting to send telepathically?

Hey, Ryder. I'm here. You're great.

CHAPTER EIGHT

I *f you keep doing things the same way, don't expect a different result.*

Remembering the numerous pep talks he'd given to himself over the past few days was the only reason Ryder didn't let his gaze slide across Carey's face and away. Besides, he'd just won a major victory — concession — whatever — with his father. What could shoot down his good mood now?

Carey could.

A woman he thought about way too often, though he'd hidden it well. Probably. But now he stayed looking at her, focusing on letting the skin around his eyes crinkle as he offered her a small smile.

She could dismiss the contact. She could fail to understand.

Instead, she held his gaze and smiled back, causing his heart to leap in his chest. Did she feel the same way he did? Really? It had been too much to hope for, but maybe... maybe this could work.

The cacophony of the Cavanagh clan converging around

Vivienne faded in the connection he felt with Carey. He took a few steps closer then shrugged internally and walked right up beside her.

"Hey." *Jeepers, Ryder.* If that wasn't a brilliant segue, he didn't know what one was.

"Hey. That's pretty cool, getting your father to hire Vivienne." Her eyes shone as she looked up at him.

"We needed a stablehand, and she needed a job."

"And you know there was far more to it than that. Sounds like this might be the big breakthrough your family needs."

Ryder held his smile as he shoved aside the reminder that Carey's father held the key to another discovery the Cavanaghs needed. That was for another day. Maybe he'd even call Branson off. Maybe it truly was water under the bridge and didn't need to be unearthed all these years later. Most likely there wasn't actually anything that needed to be dredged up, anyway.

"Yeah. It looked pretty dicey for a few minutes there. My dad is so unsettled right now, it could easily have gone either way. But you know how the Bible says, you have not because you ask not, right?"

Her smile warmed. "I've been thinking about that verse lately, too."

"So, I talked to the guys, we prayed about it, and we went for it. It will still be rocky, but it's a good start." Just a sec. She'd been thinking of James 4, too? In what context?

"Praying about situations, about decisions, is so important."

"It's vital." Was he missing something? It wouldn't be the first time. Dare he ask? *You have not, because you ask not.* Ryder took a deep breath. "What have you been praying about lately?"

Her breath caught.

If he hadn't been standing so close, — if there hadn't been a slight lull in the clan surrounding Vivienne — he wouldn't have heard it. Ryder angled his head. Waited.

"I've been praying about—"

"Carey!" Vivienne hugged her tight. "Can you believe it? This is going to be so amazing. So weird. But amazing."

Carey turned to Vivienne. "I'm so happy for you getting another shot at a relationship with your father. There's nothing like the bond between a dad and a daughter."

Ryder stilled. Of course, she loved her dad. To her, Jason Anderson was Daddy. To the Cavanagh family, he was persona non grata. At best, they didn't speak of the man. At worst, they planned to prosecute and get him tossed in jail... at least, if he deserved it. And it seemed he might.

How could Ryder, even for five minutes, entertain dreams of loving Carey? She'd have to choose between him and her dad, and what kind of stupid person was he to think he would win, no matter what a leech Jason Anderson was? The man was Carey's dad.

Ryder had fought long and hard against accepting that Declan wasn't perfect. It seemed he should always respect, obey, and adore his father. Declan had stood atop a pedestal even when Travis and Blake railed against him. Even when Adam ran away from home and joined the rodeo circuit. Even when Noah had enough and chose a life as an itinerant blacksmith instead of staying at Rockstead.

Even when Kathryn withdrew, becoming more and more silent. But when she moved into the basement suite, Ryder had to admit that something was not right in his little corner of paradise. Mentally, he'd tried to pin it on Kathryn, but the blinders had dissolved. Sure, it always took two to have a disagreement, but that didn't mean the fault lay fifty-fifty.

The problems in Dad's second marriage could be laid 95% at his own feet. Kathryn just hadn't had the backbone to stand up to her husband's bulldozing nature. At least, not until Dad's affair with Ainsley and Vivienne's mother came to light.

Why then?

It had something to do with Jason Anderson.

And Ryder's thoughts had come full circle as he refocused on Carey where she and Vivienne chatted. He took a couple of steps back.

"Ouch! Watch where you're going in those cowboy boots."

Ryder pivoted and caught Ainsley's arm. "I'm so sorry."

"Retreating already?" Her eyebrows shot up.

"Retreating?" Man, he sounded like a doofus echoing her.

"Yeah, retreating." Ainsley glanced to Carey then back at him. "Why not just admit it?"

This time he checked his spatial awareness before backing up a few more steps. "I'm not following. What am I supposed to admit?" How far was he from the door? Maybe he could make a complete escape. His interfering sister-in-law could see to it that Vivienne had a ride back to town. Carey could take her.

Travis slugged Ryder's arm. "Way to take the bull by the horns, little bro. I'm impressed."

His oldest brother's approval and praise should warm Ryder to the core, but he felt like an imposter. He didn't feel the slightest bit brave at the moment. The bold dude he'd been an hour before slinked back under the rock where it had lived most of its life. Where it deserved to live.

"Want to watch the game? Seahawks are seven-to-three

over the Steelers." Travis's elbow nudged deep. "And we have snacks."

"Oh, yeah? Cool. Sure, I can hang around for a bit." And, without a backward glance, he followed his brothers to the seating around the big screen and buried his hand in the giant bowl of potato chips.

WOULD Carey have had the nerve to tell Ryder she liked him? What had she been thinking, starting a talk like that with his entire family just a few feet away? She'd been *this* close when Vivienne had interrupted. Good thing the younger woman had come, that was all.

Carey made sure not to glance toward the football game unless cheering erupted. Then she kept it to the screen. She turned her focus on the women around the table, or at least tried to. What were they talking about? Oh, which newborn let her parents sleep better, Penelope or Oakley, and that Joseph had taken his first steps this week. Not a conversation Carey could relate to, and Taryn and Vivienne looked just as lost as she felt.

Thankfully, Ainsley soon folded the game and headed for the kitchen, but should Carey trust her friend? It would seem weird if she didn't join her, though, so she did.

"Hey, can I help with anything? The stew smells great, by the way. Is everyone staying?"

Ainsley laughed. "By which you're wondering if *Ryder* is staying."

"Shh. Don't be so loud."

"No one's nearby to overhear. Only Riley and Adam are staying after the game. I haven't invited Ryder yet, but I will."

Ainsley raised her eyebrows in a challenging manner. "Don't think I won't."

"What were you two talking about if not dinner?"

"He backed up and stepped on my foot."

Carey blinked. "He what?"

"Stepped on my foot." Ainsley stuck out her foot clad in a fuzzy pink sock with white hearts. "He's wearing boots. It hurt."

"You talked longer than that."

"You were keeping a close eye, huh?"

"Whatever."

Ainsley nudged Carey's ribs. "I was just getting started when Travis interrupted. So, you're safe. So far."

Whew. Although Ryder had been retreating from Carey when he collided with Ainsley. Maybe he did need a quick kick to the backside to keep him moving forward. But did Carey even want a man who needed to be encouraged to make the first move?

Normally, not so much. But she was smart enough to remember that he'd feel all the same reasons she did for being nervous about a relationship. He was several years younger. He was Carey's cousins' stepbrother.

Carey was done minding those trifling issues, though. The Lord knew she'd tried to excise Ryder from her mind for over a year now, and it hadn't worked. Dreams of the shy, lanky cowboy invaded both her days and her nights. She was either going to have to move away from Jewel Lake or make a serious effort to find out if she could make something out of this thing she felt for Ryder.

Maybe more exposure to him would cure her infatuation. Doubtful, but hypothetically possible.

The Steelers rebounded to win the game by a single point. The cowboys gathered around the TV groaned and began picking up their pop cans and empty bags and wrappers. Blake knelt to help his stepson, Gavin, and Travis's son, Toby, put away the wooden horses. The women tidied up behind their game and snacks as well, while Dakota shifted to an easy chair to nurse Penelope more comfortably. Oakley wailed from down the hall.

"Turn the oven to 400°?" Ainsley wiped her hands on a towel. "I need to get the baby."

"Sure." Carey tapped into the oven's control panel. "What's going in?"

"I've had a loaf of sourdough rising for dinner tonight. It's in the pantry over the vent, if you want to get it when the oven's hot."

Noah and Taryn hollered goodbye from the front door, while Dakota and Dafne sent their small sons across the ranch road at a run. The two little boys were such good friends and loved living next door to each other.

Carey glanced around. She longed to be part of a family like this one. Was the camaraderie the main appeal? The friendships between all these women who'd married the Cavanagh brothers? Or was the appeal truly the only cowboy still unattached?

Ryder stood beside Nathaniel near the fireplace. He tipped back his head and laughed at something his step-brother had said... and then his eyes focused on hers across the great room. The smile faded slightly, but the intensity grew.

Vivienne draped her arm across Carey's shoulders. "Ainsley says you're staying for dinner. Can I catch a ride back to town with you later? I didn't think about logistics when I rode up to the ranch with Ryder, and it would save him a trip all the way back."

"Of course, you may. I won't be staying too long. Morning comes mighty early when I start work at the clinic at eight."

"Yeah, I have to work tomorrow, too. My boss will be livid when I give notice for only one week, but it can't be helped. I can't stand it a minute longer. How did Dakota manage there for as long as she did?"

Carey shook her head. "I have no idea, except she had a child to support, and her parents didn't help her like Dafne's parents did. She was on her own without a career to fall back on."

"Thanks for the reminder why I want an education."

"Will your dad really pay for college?"

Vivienne shrugged. "I guess we'll see. But I should be able to save up quite a bit more without rent and groceries, and the cabins are a big improvement over being shoehorned into an apartment with Kathryn and my two sisters."

"Declan pays well?" Carey tried to keep the surprise out of her voice.

"Better than I expected, honestly."

The oven beeped. Had it come to full temperature already? "Excuse me." Carey darted into the pantry, found the rounded loaf, and tucked it into the hot oven.

Vivienne had wandered off to talk with Ryder, Nathaniel, and Adam. Bella crouched in front of little Joseph as the wobbly little guy stood beside Riley's chair. Everyone else had cleared out.

Carey turned as Ainsley returned with Oakley. "What else can I help with?"

"I think we'll go buffet style, if you wouldn't mind grabbing napkins from the pantry. I'll get Nathaniel to dig out the dishes and silverware while I nurse Oakley. Just line every-thing up on the island."

"Hey, Ainsley."

Carey startled as Ryder's voice came from close behind her, and she nearly dropped the stack of folded fabric squares.

"Hey, Ryder. Did Nathaniel invite you to stay for dinner?"

"He did. I was just checking if he had permission."

"Smart guy." Ainsley chuckled. "Yes, we'd talked about it. We'd love to have you stay."

Ryder glanced at Carey then down at his feet. "Viv says you're good with dropping her off in town later?"

"No problem. We live in the same building, after all."

"Okay. Thanks."

Ainsley stroked the baby's downy hair. "Did Nathaniel mention anything about what's going on at Sweet River Ranch to you guys?"

Ryder furrowed his brow and shook his head. "We were watching the game."

She rolled her eyes. "Men. You guys couldn't multi-task if your lives depended on it."

"Sweet River." Carey thought about it. "Isn't that the big ranch just south of the interstate? They're trying to turn it into some kind of resort, right?"

"That's the one." Ainsley leaned closer. "They sold out to an old rich guy from Chicago who's bringing in his family to run the place." She waggled her eyebrows at Carey. "By family, I mean a bunch of grandsons in their twenties and thirties. You should totally keep an eye out for these guys. They'll be moving in over the next few months to get the place ready for next tourist season."

Carey stared hard at her friend. What was Ainsley up to? Trying to embarrass her? Thanks a bunch. "Well, that should shake the community up a bit." She didn't dare glance at Ryder, not when he stood so close beside her, she could feel the heat of his arm through the sleeve of her sweater.

A timer buzzed. The baby jerked and cried. Ainsley soothed her. "Oakley's starving. Timing is everything, right? Carey, would you mind helping Bella into her booster?"

"Sure." Carey flashed a smile in Ryder's general direction and turned for the toddler.

CHAPTER NINE

The chill of the May evening caught Ryder by surprise when he followed Carey and Vivienne outside. Daytime temperatures had been pretty warm for the past week, but it felt like frost was in the air for tonight.

The season didn't much matter, nor did the weather. Ranch work went on regardless. Heat dome? Derecho? Blizzard? It didn't matter. The cows needed to be tended. The hay cut, baled, protected, doled out.

Summer was coming, which meant longer, warmer evenings and mosquitoes. They'd be haying in a few weeks. Busy times meant fewer free hours.

"Vivienne!" Ainsley called from inside as Ryder stepped out onto the deck.

His sister turned back into the house. "Yes?"

And just like that, he was alone under the starlit sky with Carey Anderson. It would probably last less than thirty seconds, but here they were. If only he weren't so undecided. So tongue-tied.

Carey shifted a little, and he could feel her presence mere inches from him. Did she have any idea what that whiff of her gardenia perfume did to him? How much it drove into his senses and made him long for things he couldn't have?

"Hey, Ryder, I was wondering if you'd like to come to my place for dinner one night this week?"

His heart stuttered as he looked down at her. "Me?" *Brilliant reply, Ry. And your voice cracked like when you were thirteen.*

"Yes, you." She nudged him with her elbow. "What evening are you free? I was thinking maybe Wednesday?"

"I..." He looked up at the sky and shot a prayer heavenward. "Me and who else?"

"Just you." She paused. "Unless you're seeing someone else or aren't interested."

Her voice had been so quiet he barely heard her words, yet they echoed back and forth inside his head. She'd really said that. Put herself out there.

What was he going to do about it? He had his reasons, but she had the same ones, most likely. If she could overlook them, couldn't he? "Are you sure?"

Carey laughed, sounding a little breathless. "You're scaring me, Ryder. Maybe I've interpreted the situation incorrectly. If so, I'm sorry." She fumbled in her purse and pulled out her keys.

He set his hand on her arm. "Carey." He was *touching* her! Well, her sweater. But still. "I didn't think..." Words. Where were they when a guy needed them in the worst way?

"Didn't think what?"

Ryder turned to face her. It was time to buck up and see where the ride would take him. Adam had made an entire career of climbing onto wild broncs and hanging on for eight seconds. A lifetime was a whole lot longer, but Adam had transitioned. Ryder could, too. Right?

"I didn't think… you would ever look at me twice." Maybe that had come out too needy. Too juvenile. Ugh. Would he ever stop reminding himself of their age difference?

"I've looked more than twice."

His blood pounded in his ears. "I have, too. Looked at you more than twice, I mean."

"So, will you come for dinner?"

The door behind them flung open, and Vivienne hurried out. "Sorry about that. I'm ready now."

Ryder could only be thankful she'd ducked back inside at all. He turned toward his sister, which meant distancing himself from Carey. "Hey, have a good week. Keep in touch, and let me know when you need help bringing your stuff up to the cabin."

"It will all fit in my car. It's not like I have furniture or anything."

"Fair enough."

Vivienne linked arms with Carey and dragged her down the steps toward the waiting vehicles.

Carey looked back over her shoulder. "See you later, Ryder. Let me know."

He cleared his throat. "The answer's yes."

Her entire face lit up. She was really beautiful in the glow of the gentle lighting from the deck.

He'd remember this snapshot in time forever.

"What's up?" Vivienne wanted to know.

Carey hip-checked her. "That's for me to know and for you to find out."

"Be that way." Viv laughed. "Man, I hope I didn't just make

the biggest mistake of my life, agreeing to work for Decl — my father."

Ryder felt the same way. Not about his half-sister moving to the ranch, but about accepting Carey's invitation to dinner. She'd expressly said she was interested in him. There'd be no deflecting when it was just the two of them.

He was interested right back. That wasn't the problem. If she didn't think the obvious reasons for holding back were strong enough, then he shouldn't, either. But... she probably didn't know he was investigating her father.

A minute later, Carey's taillights disappeared around the bend in the ranch road.

Ryder climbed into his truck and rat-a-tat-tatted his steering wheel for a minute. He had cell reception here. He wouldn't have it again until he pulled in by the corral, and Dad might come out to talk at that time. He probably regretted agreeing to hire Vivienne and would try to rescind. Then, there was no cell service over by the cabins.

His best chance at privacy was right here in the midst of Cavanaghville, as Dafne had started calling this little community of houses.

He started the truck and watched his cell signal as he drove up the road. When one bar dropped, he pulled off to the side and tapped Branson's number.

"Hey, Cav!" Branson answered immediately. "I was just going to give you a call."

"Oh? Great. Well, I'm here now. What's up?"

"You'll never believe what I found out about Jason Anderson."

Ryder's gut clenched. "About that..."

"He moved into a place right on the ocean in Maine about

a year after his brother passed away. It took a while to find the title. No mortgage on record, dude. He owns it, free and clear."

Dread sent a cold shiver down Ryder's spine. "Does that prove anything?"

"You tell me! But it's sure suspicious. Where did he get that kind of money? There seems to be only one obvious answer. I've asked a PI friend of mine to look a little deeper into Anderson's insurance agency. There's got to be some dirt in there somewhere."

An entire battle went on inside Ryder. His stepbrothers deserved answers. Closure. But he was just starting to believe that his personal happiness might be within reach. And no one had asked him to pursue Jason. No, he'd picked up the mantle all on his own.

"Ry? You still there? What did you want to tell me about? Or were you just checking up on progress, and I've answered all your questions?" Branson chuckled.

Ryder took a deep breath and clenched his free hand around the leather-wrapped steering wheel. "I was going to ask you to call everything off."

"Dude." Branson let out a belly laugh. "You can't be serious. We're finally getting somewhere. The guy's a crook. He has to be. How else could he have bought seaside property with cash when his business had been struggling only a year before?"

"I… I don't know. But my stepbrothers…" Oh, Lord. What was he supposed to do now?

"There's no way they asked you to stop now. Or they won't, once you pass on this news."

"What kind of proof do you have?"

"It's the lack of it. No loans, no mortgage trail." Branson

hesitated. "Look, I can't just let this go. You know that, right? I'm in law school. My sense of justice is wide awake and rarin' to go."

"And here I thought all lawyers were crooked."

Branson snorted. "Some may be, no doubt. But there's no class called Anti-Ethics 101. We nail down the evidence until there's absolutely no way it could add up to anything else. Hunt down any witnesses — you say the woman who worked for him back then is dead, though, right? You're sure she didn't fake her death then disappear under a new identity?"

"She's dead. She's my half-sister's mother. Vivienne went to the funeral home. Saw the casket be closed and lowered."

"Okay. If you're sure."

"I'm sure."

"And Brenda Johnson never told anyone what happened."

"Correct."

"I hate dead-ends."

"I hear you, Bran. But can we not let this go? I don't think he hurt anyone here. Not really."

"He stole their money. Well, maybe. That's what I need to figure out."

Ryder raked his mind. Had anyone ever complained of missing money? Not that he remembered. Certainly not in the vast sums that would be required for a seaside home in Maine. That wouldn't exactly be the cheapest property in the lower 48. "Can you slow it down a little?"

"What on earth are you going on about, Ryder? Do you want justice done, or don't you?"

His head was going to explode. "Not right now."

Branson mumbled some words under his breath that Ryder didn't want to remember. "I'll send you the deets in the morning. You're not going to want to drop this."

The line went dead.

Much like Ryder's emotions.

WHAT SHOULD she cook for a cowboy? They were all about beef, right? Carey couldn't broil a decent steak if her life depended on it. A roast seemed excessive for two people, but anything with ground beef seemed cheap. Pork? Chicken? Something ethnic?

Every time she made up her mind what to serve, she second-guessed herself and kept right on digging through recipe boards on Pinterest. She didn't dare ask Kathryn or Ainsley what Ryder liked. No one knew she'd invited him over. If they did, they'd certainly have commented. She wasn't going to announce it until after this first dinner... at least, if it went well.

Carey's fingers stalled out on the keyboard. Would this be considered a date? Had she really asked a man out on a *date*? Good thing Granny Wilson was long gone. And those old Regency novels would be no help. Even if a genteel lady would have been this forward, they had cooks and abigails and footmen to preserve propriety.

That was so old-fashioned. In the twenty-first century, no one would blink about a woman and a man alone in an apartment for a couple of hours. Even the pastor at Creekside Fellowship wouldn't jump to conclusions, though Mrs. McDiarmid probably would.

Okay, so, dinner. She worked until four. She'd texted him to ask if six o'clock was okay, and he'd responded hours later with a simple yes. Would there come a day when they exchanged flirty texts in rapid succession?

First, she had to cook him a dinner to remember. Then they needed to talk and determine if they were moving forward. Maybe he'd just agreed because she'd caught him flat-footed and he didn't know how to say no. But he'd admitted he'd looked at her *that way* as well.

She was totally overthinking this. What did she know how to make that she couldn't possibly flub? Burritos. Didn't every guy like them? They were a hearty dish. She could prep the components the night before then heat and assemble them when he arrived. It would give her something to do if things seemed awkward.

Things were *going* to be awkward. How could they not? She'd taken the initiative and invited a man for dinner. Not just any man, but Ryder Cavanagh.

Enough. Did she have everything she needed, or what did she have to pick up at Super One? She pulled out her recipe card, a pad of paper, and a gel pen. Let's see…

Her phone rang, and her heart jumped. Ryder? No. Laurel. "Hey, sis." She managed to keep her voice even.

"Yay, you remember who I am."

It was going to be like this? Carey nearly tapped the end button then and there. "I think we've met a time or two. Aren't you the one who's a couple of inches taller than me? Wavy blond hair. Hourglass figure. Gorgeous."

"Hardy har."

"So, how's things?"

"You said you'd call me Sunday, so we could set up a time to get together. That was yesterday."

Carey flinched. "You're right. I messed up."

"How about Wednesday? I'll even come to Jewel Lake. I've got a hankering for a Reuben from the Golden Grill."

"I can't Wednesday. How about Thursday?"

"What, you have a life?"

"Sort of. At any rate, I'm not free on Wednesday."

"It's the only night this week I can make it. How about you switch up your plans?"

"I can't." Carey ran her fingertips over the recipe card in Granny's tidy penmanship.

There was silence for a few seconds before Laurel huffed. "I wish you hadn't moved to Jewel Lake. I feel like I never see you and that you don't even care."

Laurel had taken guilt lessons from Granny Wilson. "I care."

"Wednesday?"

"I can't."

"Hot date?"

Should she tell? Not tell? "I'm not sure. It's a *first* date. I'll see whether it goes anywhere after that or not."

"Oooh, anyone I know?"

Probably? But Carey didn't want to explain Ryder to her sister. Not until she was certain they had potential. Laurel would pick at all the same negatives Carey had been dodging around for months. Right now, Carey didn't have an answer, other than she couldn't pretend she didn't care about him, regardless.

"Yeah, never mind." Laurel sighed. "It's been a lot of years since I lived in Jewel Lake. I don't really know anyone there anymore, other than our cousins. As if I even know them."

"I do see them once in a while, since Ainsley married into their family."

"Invite me sometime when they get together? If you think it would be okay?"

"I can do that. Sometimes it's pretty impromptu, though."

"Well, I guess we'll talk later. Have fun on your hot date. Kiss and tell me all about it later."

As if. "Talk to you soon."

CHAPTER TEN

It felt strange tapping the speaker button for Carey's apartment, not Kathryn's. It felt even stranger turning into the corridor onto the second floor after she'd released the lock.

Ryder's gut had been a mess for three days. On the one hand, he was thrilled to the bone that Carey felt like he did and had taken the initiative. On the other, he was absolutely terrified that they were doomed before they even started. The files Branson had sent seemed incriminating.

Carey was going to hate him.

She didn't, today.

But it was coming. It had to.

He nearly pivoted and ran back to his truck, but his boots kept moving until he stood in front of #203.

The door opened before he could knock, and Carey stood there, smiling nervously at him. Or was he projecting his anxiety on her?

He managed a smile and held out the bouquet of sweet peas and baby's breath he'd picked up at Super One, since

Petals had been closed by the time he made it off the ranch. "You look… beautiful today."

A pretty blush crept across her face as she accepted the flowers. "Thank you. You didn't have to…"

"Kathryn raised me right." Sure hadn't been his own parents.

"I'm glad to hear it. Come on in." She stepped aside, her nose buried in the flowers.

Which gave him the opportunity to study her. Her wavy brown hair brushed the shoulders of her delicate pink sweater. Jeans clung to her hips and legs, but he forced his gaze down to her feet. He chuckled at the sight of pink leather. "Nice boots."

She stuck out one foot and turned it. "You like them, huh?"

"I didn't know you were a cowgirl."

Carey looked up at him. "There's a lot you don't know."

He grinned, quelling the turbulence in his belly. "I guess that's what tonight is for. To find out if there are any deal-breakers." Besides the cards he held. He'd feel more guilty about that if he wasn't already trying to call Branson off. He'd succeed, and Carey would never need to know.

Secrets were never a good idea between couples. He knew that. But this thing would probably never get so far that they actually were a couple. A thousand things could go wrong long before the investigation came to light. Right? Right.

Ryder followed Carey into the kitchen.

She lay the flowers on the counter and stretched into an upper cupboard where he could see a crystal vase on the top shelf.

"Here. Let me." He reached past her, feeling the heat of her body against his chest as he lifted the vase down. He grinned at her. "You're short."

"Or maybe it's that you're tall," she countered, her eyebrows tilting up.

"Maybe."

Carey shifted away and poured water into the vase from the faucet. Then she tucked the bouquet inside and arranged the blooms. "There. Thank you, Ryder. They're beautiful. Want to set them on the end of the table?"

"Sure." He rounded the end of the galley kitchen into her main living area, where a small table was tucked against the kitchen wall. The place looked warm and homey in browns and pinks with gold accents here and there. Carey's style was old-fashioned, nothing like the modern aesthetic his sisters-in-law seemed to embrace or the log, stone, and antler decor in the house where he'd grown up. He liked it, though. It suited her.

The polished, dark wood table was set for two with tapered candles and elegant china and crystal that stopped his breath for a second. He was the guest that warranted this special touch? Wow.

He glanced around one more time then turned back into the kitchen. "Nice place. It's a different layout than Kathryn's." Nothing like stating the obvious.

"Right. Hers is a three-bedroom, and this has only one. But then, I don't have three teenagers living with me."

"Lucky you." He chuckled.

"I do like this building, though. It's close to downtown. Close to Creekside Fellowship. Close to the park. And the rent isn't too bad."

"You can probably walk to work."

"I often do. That's another big benefit." She stirred a pot on the stove, and the aroma of Tex-Mex seasonings filled the air.

"Mmm. What's cooking? It smells amazing." Ryder leaned over her shoulder to get a closer look.

"I thought we'd have burritos. Everything else is chopped and prepped in the fridge."

"Do you cook a lot?"

"I like to. Eating out gets old."

He didn't move away from her, though he probably should. Not only could he smell the meat-and-bean concoction, but her light floral fragrance. And then there was the tingling heat from the back of her sweater through the front of his jean shirt. Maybe someday he'd have the right to rest his hands on her hips, turn her toward him, and...

Back up, Ryder.

His brain probably meant not to let his brain run so far ahead of the current situation, but his body obeyed, too. "Can I get things out? Shall we assemble them here or at the table?"

"On the counter sounds good."

Were her cheeks pink from stirring the hot food, or from his presence? And, oh, right, her face also flushed from foods like chocolate. Good thing he'd brought flowers instead of candy.

Ryder opened the fridge and found containers of chopped lettuce, chopped tomatoes, grated cheese, and more. He laid them out along the counter while, behind him, Carey warmed tortillas in the microwave. She set two plates at the end of the buffet and glanced at him.

He took both her hands. "May I say grace?"

Carey's smile reached her eyes. "I'd like that," she said softly.

THEY'D EATEN the burritos and accompanying salad. Ryder'd had a second helping. Good sign, right? Now they lingered over salted caramel cupcakes and herbal tea — Carey would have enough trouble sleeping tonight without adding caffeine to the mix. Tension had relaxed somewhat, but it was too quiet when she could hear the faint strains of Beethoven from her Bluetooth speakers.

"Tell me five things about you that I probably don't know." All those first-date Pinterest boards had given her tools, and she wasn't afraid to use them.

Ryder leaned back in his chair, framed against the drapes covering the picture window across the space. He looked casual, fingers toying with the teacup handle, but he hadn't completely relaxed.

Carey was no stranger to dating, but she'd never been attracted to such a shy, quiet guy before. She'd never had to make the first move. She'd always been the first to realize things weren't going to work out, though. Sometimes the discord had been obvious. Other times, more subtle.

It was like her heart had been waiting for Ryder Cavanagh. But, at the moment, she wasn't certain if it was completely mutual.

"Five things, huh?"

"You're stalling."

He chuckled. "I guess so. You know a lot about me already, and I'm not particularly interesting."

"I'll be the judge of that." Carey managed to bat her eyelashes.

Ryder grinned. "Okay. Let me think. One, I like fly fishing."

"I didn't know that. Do you like cooking the fish, too?"

"I usually catch-and-release. I'm not much of a chef."

"Hmm. We might need to change that, because there's

nothing tastier than trout steamed in a foil wrap over the fire pit."

His eyebrows rose at that. "I didn't figure you for a back-woods girl."

"Not camping so much, but I love picnics and bonfires and watching the stars come out over the quiet lake."

"Me, too." Ryder's voice was quiet, his gaze intent.

Carey cleared her throat. "Second thing?"

"We should take turns as we go."

"You didn't know I liked outdoorsy stuff, so we've both done one."

"True." He narrowed his gaze. "This is hard."

She'd take pity on him if she hadn't already led in nearly every way, so she merely lifted her teacup to her lips and studied him over the rim.

"I fell off a horse the very first time I got on one. It was Travis's fault."

"How old were you?"

"Probably two or three? I don't remember it myself, but Travis and Blake love to tell the story. Travis apparently hoisted me up on his pony and slapped its rump."

"Ugh. That sounds mean."

"He was only eight or nine. But yeah, there was no real love lost between us brothers. I'd say that was the third thing, but you probably already knew."

Carey set down her teacup. "I haven't ridden often since my uncle got cancer. Before that, we sometimes went out to Running Creek, and Uncle Joe would put Laurel and me on ponies and lead us around the corral."

"That's a better way to start kids out. With adult supervision and all."

"Yes. I felt safe. And you're right, I knew you and your brothers didn't always get along."

"It's been a lot better the past few years, since Travis and Dakota made up. He was so angry all the time..." His voice trailed off.

"Anger can eat a person from the inside out."

"He was always like a bear fresh out of hibernation. Blake prodded Travis all the time then disappeared off the ranch during the fallout."

Sounded like their personalities, all right. "And you?"

Ryder shrugged. "I was a lot younger. I just held back, trying to stay out of everyone's way. Especially Dad's and Travis's."

"I'm sorry."

"Yeah, well, me, too. But like I said, it's a lot better now. Dad doesn't fly off the handle constantly. He's internalized all that stuff, which probably isn't healthy, either. He's maybe found an outlet. He and Kathryn have been getting some counseling in Missoula."

"Ainsley mentioned that. I'm glad. I hope they get things sorted out and back together."

"Me, too. It's so quiet up there now. Dad's sullen and withdrawn, Kathryn and the twins are gone, and so are all my brothers. It will be good to have Vivienne around the place."

"But you like quiet." It wasn't a question. If Ryder suddenly turned into a party-loving animal, Carey would eat her new pink cowboy boots.

"There's quiet and then there's quiet, you know? I grew up in a family of eight kids. I treasured a bit of solitude, but there was always a dull roar in the background with everyone else coming and going and arguing and laughing and whatever all."

Carey studied him as he gazed off past her like she wasn't in the room. "I'll accept that as revelation number three."

His gorgeous blue eyes refocused on her. "Oh, yeah? Then it's over to you."

"There was my sister and me, and Laurel's two years older. But we were both busy with after-school stuff. Until the divorce, anyway."

"Divorce is rough. My parents, too."

"Except, from what I've heard, your parents fought all the time. Ours didn't. I had no clue anything was wrong. I mean, Dad was at work a lot, but I was just a little kid. I didn't know how much was normal."

If it wasn't a trick of the candlelight, Ryder seemed to be studying her even more intently.

"My dad wasn't anything like his brother. Uncle Joe was gentle and devoted to Aunt Kathryn and his kids. My dad… less so."

"Do you still see him much? I mean, my mother moved back to Jewel Lake, but I've only seen her a couple of times. She mostly stays out of Dad's way, except for showing up at Blake and Dafne's wedding. You were there, right? It was super awkward."

Carey reached over the table and covered his hand. He was adorable when he was nervous. "Yeah, I noticed. My dad moved out of town, and I don't see him often. He hasn't been back to Montana in probably ten, fifteen years. Not even for my high school graduation. My sister and I have gone out there a couple of times."

"Carey, I—"

She didn't want his pity. "All I know for sure is that, when — or if — I get married, I want to make sure the guy is the right one for me. That we're on the same page spiritually and morally and all that. Because I don't want to get divorced. I don't want to do that to my kids. To myself."

Ryder nodded and closed his eyes for a second before looking at her again. "I totally agree. Travis didn't want to get married because he could see our dad in himself. With all the anger problems, you know? He figured it was better to send Toby back and forth every weekend than to take the risk going all-in with Dakota."

"They seem okay now." Travis was so sweet with his newborn daughter.

"And then Blake was the opposite. He figured he'd just never get serious with anyone. He'd be a perpetual Peter Pan with a never-grow-up mindset."

"Which worked until he met Dafne." Carey smiled at the thought of the pair of them. She'd gotten to know Dafne some over the past while, since Blake's girlfriend — now wife — had hit it off with Ainsley.

Ryder chuckled. "Yeah. She doesn't take any nonsense out of him, but he doesn't seem to mind."

Carey took a deep breath. "So, what about you?"

"Me?"

He might give her the innocent wide-eyed look, but he wasn't fooling her. He knew what she meant. "You."

"Marriage scares me. I've always figured that was because I was so young."

"Pfft."

Ryder blinked then laughed. "It's true, though. I'm only twenty-four."

"When's your birthday?"

"August eighth."

"We'll have to do something special that day. Birthdays

should be celebrated." Would they still be together in three months? Or even next week?

"I know you're Ainsley's age. So… twenty-eight?" He gestured between them. "Does the difference bother you?"

Time for honesty. "It did at first, yeah. But the more I hung around your family and you, the more I realized it really didn't matter. It's not like you're fourteen and I'm eighteen."

He grinned just a little. "But we once were."

"So, it bugs you that I'm older?"

"I'm trying to get over it, because I really like you, Carey. I tried super hard to talk myself out of it, but it didn't work."

Lay out all the cards. "And then there's the family connection. That you're my cousins' step-brother."

"That, too. We're practically family."

"But not."

Ryder held her gaze. "But not."

She set her teacup down on its saucer, clinking a little extra hard. Darn nerves. Then she met his gaze.

He laid both his hands on the table, palms up. "Where do we go from here?"

Carey placed her hands against his warm ones, feeling the strength in both his grip and in his dark gaze. "Forward. If you want to."

"I definitely want to."

CHAPTER ELEVEN

Y ou're more spaced out than usual." Blake swung a saddle onto Zorro's back and glanced over at Ryder.

Ryder tightened Champlain's cinch. "Really?" He *felt* high on something. He'd barely slept a wink and now it seemed his boots floated above the uneven surface of the corral.

"Must've been a hot date last night. Finally taking my advice and putting yourself out there, huh?"

Ryder straightened, gathered the reins together, and mounted his gelding.

"Dude." Blake laughed. "In case you've never noticed, the only way to drive off the ranch is right past our house. Dafne saw you go out around five-thirty, and you didn't come back until nearly eleven. Where'd you go?"

"Cavanaghville's in a dumb place, then, if you guys have nothing better to do than spy on others."

"It's not like Dad goes anywhere, unless he still hangs out with his cronies on Sunday mornings when the rest of us are in church. That leaves you. And I wouldn't call it spying so much as being observant of our surroundings. There are little kids living there, and we have to keep aware in case mountain lions or grizzlies or what have you prowl close to the houses."

"It's not like bears come with headlights."

"Exactly!" Blake looked smug. "So, we were pretty sure it wasn't Smokey or Bruno driving by."

Ryder rolled his eyes. "Get on your horse. It's time to ride out."

Their job today was scouting the lower pastures to check when the cows and calves could be moved onto fresh grass. Couldn't come soon enough for Ryder. The hayshed had nearly emptied, and they'd soon be mowing this year's first cut. A breather in between would be most welcome.

"I've got all day to badger you, you know."

"Get a life."

Blake opened the gate and led Zorro through it, waited for Ryder and Champlain, closed it again, and mounted up. "I've definitely got a life, and I like it quite a lot, to be honest."

Probably more information than Ryder wanted to hear.

"I'm not going to let it go. Where were you last night?"

"Town."

"Well, duh. Do I need to tell you what else I know?"

Uh oh. Ryder's gut chilled. "Not sure..."

"Alexia saw your truck in the parking lot. Saw you walking up to the building. She was sure you'd come to see her and Em and Kathryn. When you didn't show up, she got to wondering where you might've gone instead."

"She sounds like a regular Sherlock Holmes." A blabby one. Ryder nudged Champlain into a trot as they headed up toward the meadows.

"Carey Anderson, huh?"

He closed his eyes for a few brief seconds, searching for a brilliant answer. A believable denial.

"Which leaves me to wonder. Are you digging up dirt on her dad? Or are you courting her?"

"Shut up, Blake."

"Valid question, I think. Whatever went on back then, it wasn't Carey's problem. She's cool. Dafne likes her a lot."

"I know her father isn't her fault."

"And you'd never use her to get at him."

Ryder yanked on Champlain's reins, spun the horse to face Blake, and poured all his frustration into his voice. "Is that what you think of me?"

"Peace, bro." Blake held up his hand. "Just saying this vendetta against Jason is longstanding. But I've seen how you look at Carey—"

"Right. There's been nothing to see."

"So why were you at her place last night for three or four hours?"

Ryder took a deep breath and willed his frustration to dissipate as he exhaled. "We had dinner. Talked."

"About her father?"

"She mentioned him once. That wasn't the purpose, regardless of what your pea-brain came up with."

"No, my pea-brain figures you've fallen for her hook, line, and sinker. But then there's that nagging bit in the back of my brain that remembers you're investigating her father."

"It's complicated."

"My brain isn't so tiny that it can't navigate complex theories. Try me."

A vee of Canada geese flew north, honking at each other

companionably, small, flapping dots against a brilliant blue sky. The aspens and birches along the trail seemed lit from within by their new growth. The mountain air was crisp and clean, last night's frost a faint memory as the sun warmed the trail.

"Ryder?"

He took another deep breath. "I like her. A lot." He shot a glance toward his brother. Where was the *gotcha* glee? Not there. "And, yeah, that's a problem. I called Branson a couple of days ago — Sunday evening, actually — and told him to forget it. You guys have said all along that the odds were mighty slim of finding anything worth knowing, anyway."

"Whew." Now Blake did grin. "So, Branson's off the case."

"I wish."

"What do you mean?"

"He'd just found something he's sure is evidence and got a PI friend on it."

"But you called him off."

"His sense of justice, as he called it, won't let him let it go."

Blake whistled. "Oh, boy."

"Yeah."

"You're in over your head, kid."

"Trust me. I figured that part out all by myself."

Blake shifted in his saddle and glanced over. "So... what are you going to do?"

"Pray a lot. Hope for the best."

"You mean ride your runaway and hope you don't tumble over a cliff."

"I believe I mentioned praying."

"Dude. There's a time for praying and a time for hauling back on the reins. What outcome are you looking for? Seriously?"

Ryder's mouth moved before his brain did. "Carey."

"Then you have to convince Branson to cease-and-desist. You can't have it both ways."

But what if he *could* have it both ways? What if Carey would be just as relieved as the Cavanagh family — okay, Ryder — to have her father brought to justice? Or, what if the investigation cleared Jason's name completely? Wouldn't it be better to know?

And even if Jason was guilty as sin, wouldn't Carey want closure?

He thought about his own father. Would he want to know if Declan had done something illegal? If Declan had hurt someone else's family? Because he *had* taken advantage of Brenda Johnson. Sure, he'd supported the resulting baby — Vivienne — but he'd covered it up for the better part of two decades.

No. Ryder was pretty sure he'd want to know. That meant Carey would, too. She wouldn't see it as invading her personal privacy or exposing someone — some*thing* — she'd rather keep hidden.

In that case, he should just tell her what he'd done. What Branson had found. How he'd asked Branson to stop but been thwarted.

"Be honest with her," Blake said quietly. "Nothing good comes from keeping secrets."

Blake wasn't wrong, but the timing was. Didn't there need to be some kind of tipping point where one side clearly outweighed the other? Because now, it could still easily go either way.

Ryder shifted in his saddle. "I will. Soon."

That decision should come as a relief. Funny how it didn't.

CAREY SAT across from Stephanie Simpson in a booth at the Golden Grill. It was lunchtime on Friday, and this had become their regular meetup, since they both had an hour-long break from work.

Ainsley hadn't said a word to her about the dinner date with Ryder, which almost certainly meant Ryder hadn't said anything to his brothers. Which meant... what, exactly? That he was keeping it to himself. He was a private person, so it shouldn't be too surprising.

Carey was a private person, too, but this thing with Ryder? She was exploding from holding it in. She squeezed the lemon wedge into her ice water and eyed Stephanie. "Can you keep a secret?"

Stephanie's eyes widened. "Oooh, tell me!"

"That didn't answer my question." Carey had to laugh at her friend's enthusiasm, anyway.

"Of course, I can."

The server set two giant plates heaped with Southwest Salad in front of them. "Is there anything else I can get for you girls?"

Carey sniffed the blackened chicken breast appreciatively. This was her favorite meal of the week. Except for Wednesday's date — it had been a date, right? "This is great, thanks."

"I'm good." Stephanie smiled at the woman. "Thank you."

As soon as the server turned away, Stephanie looked at Carey again. "Time to tell all."

It would be a relief to get a break from hearing about Stephanie's worries about the youth pastor. Eli hadn't asked her out for over a week. They hadn't been hanging out. Stephanie was desperately trying to hold on.

How could Stephanie be so determined to keep a guy who clearly wasn't into her as much as she was into him? Was Carey guilty of the same thing, pushing Ryder until he capitulated?

She glanced around to be sure no one was in hearing range before leaning forward. "I invited a guy over for dinner the other night."

Stephanie's eyes widened. "You did *not*."

"Sure did."

"Who? Oh, wait. Don't tell me. Let me guess." She tapped her chin as she studied Carey.

Was this what animals in a lab felt like? Because Carey felt distinctly uncomfortable. She spooned salsa across the salad and dolloped sour cream before Stephanie nodded.

"One of the Sullivan grandsons? If I weren't totally in love with Eli, I'd give a try for one of those hot cowboys myself. Which one?"

"The who?"

"Sweet River Ranch. You heard about that — you didn't? Oh. My. Word. Those guys are total hunks. The previous owners tried to expand into a resort for the past few years, but they were always strapped for cash." Stephanie folded her napkin, her mouth pressed into a tight line.

She worked at the bank and probably knew far too much about everyone's financials. Besides, Carey couldn't care less about the old or new owners of Sweet River. She opened her mouth to say so, but Stephanie kept going.

"So, this rich old guy from Chicago bought it. If he's not a billionaire, he must be close. Just snapped up that entire ranch like it was a bite of poached egg. Now he's bringing in his grandsons — did I mention they're single? And hot?"

Carey laughed. "You did mention that."

"Anyway, if you didn't know, it wasn't one of them. So, who *did* you invite for dinner?"

She took a bite of salad to forestall having to answer. Was Stephanie truly trustworthy? Her biggest fault seemed to be being in love with being in love. As far as Carey could tell, Stephanie's love life was on the rocks. Maybe if Eli broke up with her, she'd switch focus to one of the new cowboys.

"Carey?"

"Ryder Cavanagh."

"Oooh!" Stephanie squealed, pressing her hand to her heart. "He's so cute and adorable. But…"

Carey eyed her friend. "But, what?"

"Isn't he a little young for you?"

"Why does it matter? It's not like he's still in high school or something. We're both adults."

"No, but a man should be two years older than his wife, ideally."

"Are you serious? Where did you get that?"

"It just makes sense."

"Does not." Carey shook her head. She'd been doing some figuring of her own. "Women generally live longer than men, so marrying a younger man means it's less likely for the woman to be widowed for a long time."

"I guess that's true." Stephanie took a bite of her salad. "I never thought of it that way. How much older are you?"

"Three and a half years."

"I'm sorry. That still seems like a lot."

"He's very nice." Total understatement.

"Yeah, he seems like it — and we've already established that he's cute — but he's just a cowboy, right?"

Carey's back stiffened. "So are the guys you were just mooning over at Sweet River."

"No. They're career men who came here at their grandfather's bidding. Maybe to get a piece of his wealth when he passes."

"And being mercenary is a recommendation? I doubt Eli makes a ton of money as a youth pastor."

Stephanie grimaced. "You're right about that, but Cavanaghs are rich, too."

Were they? Carey had never heard rumors of that sort. They did own the largest ranch in the area, and that main house was humungous — not that she'd ever been inside — but they didn't flaunt money. She'd never really thought about it beyond that they didn't seem to be hurting financially. Neither was she. She definitely wasn't rich, but she lived within her means as a physical therapist, and it was enough. She was comfortable.

Would she like more money? Sure. Who wouldn't? But was that why she was attracted to Ryder? Not even a little bit. "Ryder's a good guy. He's sweet. He works hard. He's quiet and shy, which is amazing all by itself in a family that size."

"You've thought this through. You really like him."

"I've been hung up on him for over a year, and it seemed like he noticed me, too. One of us had to finally take the first step."

"You?" Stephanie's eyebrows hiked. "My parents would have a fit if I did that. They're so old-school."

Carey's parents didn't know. Mom might or might not care, and who knew about Dad? He'd likely flip out no matter who Carey was interested in, but a Cavanagh would be the worst. Well, she simply wouldn't tell him until she could flash a diamond in his face.

"Do you think...?" Stephanie stabbed lettuce onto her fork.

"What?"

"I'm worried about Eli ever since Harper Satterfield took over in the church office for Mrs. McDiarmid. She's really pretty and, well, nice. And Eli seems rather distant lately."

"I'm sorry to hear that."

"I don't know what to do. My parents are sure Eli will propose soon. Dad thinks I'd be a great pastor's wife, you know? I was over the moon when Eli asked me out back in February. But lately, I'm not so sure it's going to work out."

Carey cringed on the inside, but hopefully it didn't show. "It's hard to like a guy and not be sure if he likes you back." Wasn't that the truth?

"I just don't get it. Am I so unlovable?"

"No." That was an easy, quick response, but it was valid. "I wouldn't hang out with you if I didn't think you were a great person. I'm happy to be your friend."

"Thanks." Stephanie stabbed her fork into her salad. "That's how I feel about Harper, too. She's nice. Eli could do much worse, but why? He already has me. I care about him so much, but it doesn't seem to be enough for him."

Spending so much time watching Stephanie yearn for Eli had made Carey realize she didn't want to waste another year waiting for Ryder to decide if he would or wouldn't pursue her.

Carey wasn't going to be the woman everyone talked about the way they'd talked about Stephanie and probably would again. And Ryder had, in fact, come for dinner. They'd talked for several hours and gotten to know each other. They'd agreed that they both wanted to move forward. He'd texted her a sweet thank-you the next afternoon.

So, why wasn't she over-the-moon excited to tell the world she and Ryder were an item? Was it only because he hadn't kissed her when he said goodnight? Only because he hadn't seemed to tell anyone himself? That she knew people would react like Stephanie had, with a reminder of their age difference?

Or was there another reason she felt like she was waiting for the other shoe to drop?

CHAPTER TWELVE

W hat's got you in such a good mood? It's like you're actually floating, though I can hear your boots hitting the concrete." Vivienne leaned on her rake in Champlain's stall.

"Floating?" Ryder raised one eyebrow at his sister, but his attempt at being serious failed when he couldn't help but grin as well.

"Pretty much."

"Uh… it's a beautiful spring day. What's not to like?"

"Ryder. I'm not stupid."

"I didn't say you were."

"So, what's going on? I thought we'd hang out more in the evenings now that I live up here, but you seem to be spending a lot of time in town. More than I ever expected of you, frankly."

He slipped the halter over Champlain's twitching ears. "I'll be meeting Adam and Nathaniel soon to move cows into that lower pasture. Maybe I'm just happy to be done feeding them for the summer."

"Which totally accounts for why you're off the ranch evenings. Scouting the pastures in your truck rather than on the ATV or on horseback? Somehow, I don't think so."

Ryder eyed his sister.

She eyed him back then her eyebrows tilted up. "Emma and Alexia might have tattled."

"Uh…" He should have thought of them.

"Carey Anderson, huh?"

If only there wasn't a flush creeping up his neck and across his cheeks. "They have nothing better to do than spy out the window?"

"So, it's true then? You're at her apartment every evening?"

"Not *every* evening."

"You two are dating?"

Was it dating when they hadn't been out anywhere in public? When he hadn't held her hand — other than during grace before a meal — or kissed her? He definitely needed to kiss her soon. He wasn't a first-date kisser, but were the evenings they'd spent together actually dates? Maybe he needed to brave up and take her out somewhere.

"Ryder, it's a simple question with a simple answer. Are you dating Carey Anderson? Yes or no will suffice."

He took a deep breath. "I really like her. A lot. For right now, we're just getting to know each other to see where it goes. We don't need all my siblings in our business during this stage."

"Too late, bro."

Ryder pivoted to see Adam leaning on the gatepost, Nathaniel right behind him. Both guys wore amused smirks. What had they overheard? Too much.

"Carey, huh?" Adam wandered in. "As in, our cousin Carey."

Ryder's back stiffened. "*Your* cousin, bro. Not mine."

"Good point. Why did I not see this coming?"

Vivienne scoffed. "Because guys are blind. I've heard all about how you and Riley pretended to be engaged and pretended not to be falling in love with each other. I don't think you can claim to be the brightest lightbulb in the box."

"She's got you there." Nathaniel smirked. "On the other hand, I get why you'd want to keep things quiet for a while. Just make sure you don't fall into the same trap I did. It's better to get out in public more, even if it's in Missoula where the family won't see you together."

"I won't get her pregnant, bro. I haven't even kissed her."

Vivienne rolled her eyes. "Too much information. From all of you."

Nathaniel shook his head. "It took two of us to make that baby, Vivienne. If you don't know how that happens, maybe we should sit down and have a talk, because one of these days some dude is gonna come along and sweep you off your feet, and I don't want you getting hurt."

"I'm not planning on dating anyone for, like, ten years. I'm too scarred from my messed-up childhood and my father's rejection to want to go there. Besides, I have at least four years of college to get through and then I want to work and travel and do things before I settle down."

"Famous last words," muttered Adam. "Seeing the world isn't all it's cracked up to be."

At least the spotlight was off of Ryder for now. "It's good to have goals, Viv. And there's nothing wrong with dating casually. Unless you consider Blake. He was three-timing his girlfriends for a while there, thinking no one could get hurt if everything was open and visible."

"That didn't work out so well for him," Nat put in. "Until Dafne caught his attention, anyway."

"Right." Adam widened his stance, tucked his thumbs in his belt loops, and eyed Ryder. "But I think we were talking about Ryder here. And while he's apparently growing up, I can't help but be concerned knowing you're investigating her father. You're in over your head, kid. Nothing good can come from attempting both those at the same time, with the same woman."

Nathaniel looked between them. "Maybe Ryder talked to her about that?"

That darn flush again.

Adam pinned Ryder with his dark gaze. "Sorry. My mistake if you've been open, and it's all still good."

"I... haven't."

"Dude!" Adam huffed. "Get your head screwed on straight. That's my cousin you're messing with. If you're pretending to like her just so you can scope out her father, that's beyond insulting."

"That's not how it is."

"Explain."

"I like her. A lot. I have for a couple of years now, since she moved back to Jewel Lake. But it seemed dumb, you know? I mean, she's nearly four years older than me..."

"I can do math," Adam said grimly. "Keep talking."

"And I know she's your cousin, so she's almost family." Ryder would ignore Adam's eye roll. "And yeah, there's that whole thing with her dad. So, it's complicated."

Adam huffed. "Call Branson off, dude."

Nathaniel shook his head. "But you still need to tell her about it, because that's not the kind of secret that's good for a marriage."

"Who said anything about getting married?" But, oh, that argument sounded weak, even to Ryder's own ears.

"If marriage isn't your endgame, get out now." Adam made a disgusted noise. "I can't believe I have to tell you this, but learn from my mistakes. Don't date unless you can see the hope of a lifetime with the woman in question. I know Blake and I aren't the best examples, but you don't have to be like us. Value the women in your life. It might not work out. I get that. But at least treat her honestly in the meanwhile."

"Long speech," Vivienne commented.

Adam wrinkled his nose at their sister. "You can take my message to heart, too, kid."

Was Nathaniel right? Did Ryder have to come clean with Carey over this? His gut soured. He probably did. His reluctance to do so was likely why he hadn't kissed her yet.

What did he want more? Justice for his stepmother and stepbrothers? Or Carey?

Carey. Hands down. And not just because the investigation wasn't anything Kathryn or her sons had asked for.

Because the more time he spent with Carey, the stronger the feelings he had for her.

He'd have to make a decision. Soon. But was it so wrong to bask in this peaceful time in their relationship before dropping his bomb?

Another week or two couldn't hurt.

"Want to go into Missoula for dinner on Friday?" Ryder stood so close, looked at her so intently. "I was thinking of taking you to The Meating Place and then to the Roxy for the music festival."

Carey caught her breath. "Um, that's my mom and step-dad's restaurant." Going out together in public was one thing, but starting out there seemed loaded with pressurize.

"Oh. We could go somewhere else?"

"And my sister and her boyfriend are going to the music festival."

"It sounds like you don't want your family knowing we're seeing each other." Ryder chewed on his lip, his expression a little disappointed.

"Does your family know?"

He nodded. "Some of them, anyway. The girls know. Most of my brothers do."

"Oh. You hadn't told me that."

"It's new." He huffed a breath. "Okay, so Adam and Nathaniel came in on Vivienne cornering me in the stable a couple of days ago. That's how they found out. Of course, they were full of brotherly advice."

"I'm sure." Carey narrowed her gaze at him, but she couldn't call him on the situation, since she'd been carefully keeping things to herself, except for Stephanie. As far as she could tell, Stephanie had kept her secret.

Ryder took Carey's hands in his and tugged her closer.

She went willingly then pulled her hands free to set them on his shoulders, where she toyed with the collar of his snap-front shirt. She peered up at him through her lashes. How was he with subliminal text? *Kiss me, Ryder.*

His strong hands rested on her hips.

That was a good start. She let her fingers trail up his neck and across his smooth jaw. He'd shaved before he'd come to town, like usual. He didn't always when he was visiting his stepmom, so she knew it was for her. But wasn't it a waste if they never kissed?

"Carey." His voice was low. Needy.

"Hmm?" She tilted her face to look at him.

Ryder's hands smoothed the back of her T-shirt, cradling her closely.

Yes! This was more like it. He bent his head slightly, and there he was, only an inch or two away, his eyes questioning. Then he brushed his lips against hers.

Her senses exploded at the brief touch.

Ryder groaned and pulled her tighter, his lips on hers. For someone inexperienced in dating as he'd professed, he sure knew how to kiss. Not that she was an expert, though this wasn't her first. But with Ryder, it seemed easy. Right. Perfect, even.

His lips roved hers until her legs could barely keep her upright. She clung to his shoulders and gave him back kiss for kiss.

It seemed forever and yet no time at all when he pulled back. His strong hand cupped the back of her head and pressed it into the curve of his shoulder, and his lips branded her forehead with one perfect nuzzle.

Wow.

"Carey, I hope I didn't take advantage of you. I just... I just don't want to push you."

"I wanted you to kiss me," she murmured against his shirt. "I've wanted it forever."

His hands tightened, if that were even possible. "Me, too. You're everything I hoped for. I know I'm young, but..."

Carey pressed a finger against his soft lips. "Let's not talk about age anymore, okay?"

Ryder kissed her finger. "If you're sure."

"I'm sure. I mean, I know it's real, but it honestly doesn't matter. Not anymore."

"Okay. If you say so."

"I say so."

He kissed her forehead again and, as nice as that felt, it seemed like a waste of lip movement when he could be kissing her mouth.

Carey stretched her arms then brought her hands around his head to cradle it, sinking her fingers into his short hair. "Kiss me?"

His eyes crinkled and the ends of his mouth tipped up. "If you say so."

"I say so."

Ryder's lips descended on hers, this time less urgently, more exploratory.

Was this cowboy for real? Because Carey could see a bright future spread out in front of them, where kisses like these might be the punctuation to every conversation, every meal, every time they neared each other.

When they finally broke for air a second time, Ryder rested his forehead against hers. "I'm ready to go public if you are."

Most of his family already knew. What did going public mean to him?

"Sit with me in church? Come to the Golden Grill with the crew afterward?"

Once they'd been together at the Golden Grill, the entire town would know. The owner, Estelle Mulligan, was the worst gossip. Well, next to Creekside Fellowship's church secretary, Mrs. McDiarmid. That pair would certainly spread the news like wildfire.

Did it matter? Because hadn't Carey already decided Ryder was worth risking for? She wouldn't have invited him for dinner a couple of weeks ago if she'd thought they'd keep it a secret forever. That was no way to live long term.

"Okay." The word popped out on a breath and was rewarded with a long, slow kiss. She finally pulled back enough to break the contact. "And you're right about my family. Why don't I ask my mom to hold us a table Friday evening? Then she won't be caught blindsided when I come in with you."

Ryder's eyes searched hers. "Are you sure?"

"I'm sure. There's nothing at all wrong with our relationship. I've just been used to cradling these thoughts close to my heart and enjoying the sweet secrecy. But it's not because I'm ashamed of you, Ryder Cavanagh. It's because I'm a private person."

"What will your parents think?"

"Does it matter?" She touched his lips with her finger. "My dad's not around, and my mom's cool. I'll tell her, and I'm sure she'll understand. Love doesn't appear on demand, you know. It finds its own path."

She stared into his shocked eyes. Had she really used the L-word? Heat flared up her cheeks. "What I meant to say was—"

"I know what you meant." Ryder captured her hands between them, giving air a tiny chance to flow. "It's..."

"Too early, I know." But Carey knew what she felt. She'd been on a lot of first dates and a bunch of second and third ones, as well. She'd never felt like this about anyone else. Never. But Ryder didn't have her experience, not with how secluded his life had been, to say nothing of his age. Which she wasn't going to think about anymore.

"Barely too soon." Ryder's words were all but a whisper. "There's definitely something there, something worth pursuing. I want you to know, I'm not the sort of guy who kisses and makes light of it. I really see the potential of something... long term... with you."

"I know. I do, too." She smiled up at him. "I trust you, Ryder." *With my whole heart.* But it wasn't surprising he wasn't quite there yet. This thing between them had only been acknowledged for a couple of weeks. There was no rush to make declarations and promises.

"So... dinner Friday?"

"I'd love that."

CHAPTER THIRTEEN

The twins were at youth group. Vivienne was up at Rockstead. Still, Ryder lingered in front of their apartment door. If Carey planned to tell her mom, then he needed to talk to Kathryn. At one time, the two women had been married to brothers. It felt wrong for Carey's mom to know, but not Kathryn. It wasn't even a matter of if the women shared information. As far as Ryder knew, Kathryn and Ellen weren't close. Hadn't been since Joe's death, at least.

But that really had nothing to do with it. Kathryn was the closest thing to a mother Ryder had. Monica didn't count, not the way she'd stormed out when he was just a little kid and only surfaced a couple of times since. Neither time had she tried to create a relationship with her youngest son.

No. Kathryn was Ryder's mom. And... also Carey's aunt. He took a deep breath and rapped firmly on the door.

Footsteps approached. A few seconds later the door edged open and his stepmother's surprised face looked back at him. "Ryder? You didn't buzz or call. Sorry, I wasn't expecting you."

"I... can I come in for a few minutes? I need to talk to you."

"Sure." She widened the opening and gestured down at her pajama pants and baggy T-shirt covered in neon pink hearts. "I wasn't expecting company."

"Sorry. I should have texted, at least."

"Well, you're here now. Come on in. The girls will be home in about a half hour."

He trailed into the apartment Kathryn shared with the twins. They'd even wedged Vivienne in for over a year after Ainsley's marriage to Nathaniel. If anyone knew how to take the long view and forgive those who hadn't even asked for it, Kathryn did. Imagine taking in one's spouse's illegitimate, hidden child. Ryder wasn't sure he would have a big enough heart.

"Can I make you coffee? Tea?"

Ryder shook his head. "No, thanks." He closed the door then doffed his cowboy hat and twisted it between his hands. "I just wanted you to know that Carey and I are dating."

Kathryn's eyebrows rose and an amused smile toyed with her mouth. "Carey Anderson? My niece?"

He swallowed hard. "Yes. That Carey."

"You two are finally admitting your attraction?" Kathryn wiped the back of her hand across her forehead in an exaggerated motion of relief.

"I... uh... you knew?"

She chuckled. "Sit down, Ryder. You're so tall, you're putting a crick in my neck looking up at you. And of course, I knew. The girls were messing with you two back a few weeks ago with that gingerbread cake, so I was watching both of you closely. It was entertaining, to say the least."

Well, wasn't that nice? Being someone's entertainment, all

unawares. He took a seat in the easy chair nearest the door. "You don't think it's weird?"

"Why would I?"

"Because she's older than me, and because we're sort of related." He'd leave his third reason off, because he wasn't sure Kathryn was aware of his investigation into Jason Anderson.

"Age is just a number, Ryder. I think you've figured that out." Kathryn settled on the sofa nearby.

He nodded.

"And, since there's no blood between you and Carey. It's not like there'd be a potential problem with your offspring's genetics."

Ryder tried to keep his eyes from widening. He hadn't thought as far as kids. He just knew that some would think they were too closely related even though facts said they weren't. "So, you're okay with me dating Carey?"

"Of course. She's a lovely girl. I'm thankful she moved back to Jewel Lake and into this building so I could get to know her again as an adult, not just the little kid who got yanked around between her parents at their divorce."

"Her parents fought over her and Laurel?" This was news to him.

"Briefly." Kathryn shook her head. "There at the end, Jason was flailing every which way, trying to make his mark."

Ryder leaned closer. "Oh? I remember hearing he proposed to you."

She raised her eyebrows at him. "I know you know more than that, or you wouldn't be investigating him."

"You heard about that, huh?" He scratched his ear.

"I don't live under a rock, Ryder. Why didn't you just ask me if he'd done anything illegal?"

"I know he tried to."

"He wanted an easy road to wealth. He eyed Joe's life insurance policy. He eyed Running Creek Ranch. He figured Joe owed him something."

"But you married my father instead."

Kathryn let out a breath. "I did. And I'd do it again in a heartbeat, even without the need to send a strong message to my former brother-in-law."

Wait. What? "You love my dad?"

Her lips twisted to one side. "Is that so hard to believe?"

They were getting way off track here, but didn't Ryder already have the answer to his most important question? "He's not an easy man to love."

"No, he isn't. He's built up some walls, but they're slowly coming down. I think he's making progress."

"Really?" Ryder tried not to put any hope into that single word, but it was difficult to resist.

"Really. I'm praying him into the kingdom, Ryder. And I'm praying restoration into our marriage."

"I pray for you, too. All of us guys do."

"I know. Thank you." She twisted her hands in her lap. "Ryder, I do have one concern. You need to let this thing with Jason go. Whatever he tried to do to the boys and me, he didn't succeed."

"But Branson has found out Jason paid cash for an ocean-side place in Maine. Doesn't that seem suspicious?"

"There are many ways Jason could have come across money, some of them quite legal. Maybe he bought a winning lottery ticket."

"Or maybe he succeeded in fleecing someone else."

"Ryder, if you have any actual proof, take it to the police and then back out of it. This isn't a situation for an amateur sleuth, especially one who is dating the subject's daughter. You can't have it both ways, my son."

"I know. I told Branson to let it go, but he's like a dog with a bone and won't give up. He keeps emailing me stuff."

"Ryder."

"I know, but I don't know what to do. I can't seem to stop him."

"How hard have you really tried?"

He sighed as he looked down at his boots. "Not enough, I guess, when you put it that way."

Kathryn rested her hand on his forearm. "I'm not saying Jason is above board in his choices. I'm not saying it's not possible that someone else was hurt by him, just because we weren't, no matter how hard he tried. I'm saying it's not your job to do this. You're not a victim, you're not the police, and you're not someone withholding information. You're a... a bystander. And, Ryder? You don't have anything to prove to me or Adam or Noah or Nathaniel. We know you care." She squeezed his arm. "I love you, Ryder. You don't have to buy that love. You've had it ever since you crawled into my lap as a six-year-old needing a mama."

Words caught in Ryder's throat. He tried to swallow them out of the way, but something kept clogging his airways. Finally, he managed to stammer out, "Thanks."

"I'm only sorry all you boys — and your sisters — got caught up in the drama between your father and me. But, even though it affects all of you, it's between us, okay? It's not up to you to fix things for others. You're free to pursue Carey. To love her. To marry her, if that's what's coming."

Ryder's eyes blurred a little as he squeezed his stepmom's hand on his arm. "I can't tell you what that means to me."

"I got bogged down there for a few years. I'm sorry my

depression impacted you so much. I couldn't see it then, but I see it now. I see *you*."

He'd felt so bereft when Kathryn drifted away, first emotionally and mentally, then physically. She'd held on enough to homeschool the twins, but he'd missed so much, personally. How could he even think about loving someone the way she deserved? He didn't know how.

Panic swelled, but he pushed it back down. God hadn't let him down thus far and wasn't likely to start now. He needed to be in the Word more. Cling to his Savior when humans didn't make sense. He could break the chain of a poor example like his brothers had done. Kathryn's sons likely remembered their parents loving each other, but even Travis and Blake had managed to build something beautiful and worthwhile with the women they loved.

He could do it, too. And he'd start by getting it through Branson's thick skull that he was no longer interested in hearing about Jason Anderson's exploits.

"To what do I owe the honor of this meeting?" Mom searched Carey's eyes as they hugged. "You're not in trouble, are you?"

Carey's back stiffened. "No, of course not. I just had some-thing to tell you, and I thought it would be easier in person. That's why we're meeting here." She gestured to the riverfront walk along the Clark Fork. The east side of Missoula was nearly equidistant between Jewel Lake and Mom and Frank's place.

"You're still scaring me."

"Sorry, I didn't mean to." Carey took a deep breath. This

would be like ripping off an adhesive bandage, right? "I'm dating someone."

"Well, the Lord be praised. It's about time."

"Mom!"

"Seriously. Laurel is thirty and you're twenty-eight. I'd nearly given up hope of grandchildren."

"I'm *dating* someone. I'm not married or pregnant."

"It's a good start. Who is he? Anyone I'm likely to know? Although it's been a lot of years since I moved out of Jewel Lake."

Here went nothing. "Yes, it's someone you know." Carey sent a quick prayer into the blue. "Ryder Cavanagh."

"Ryder? *Cavanagh?*"

It was like each part of his name was a separate question. And maybe they were. "Yes."

Mom's mouth opened and closed several times before she shook her head. "And it's not even April Fool's Day."

"I wouldn't kid you about something like this. Ryder and I have been interested in each other for a long time, and we've been hanging out for a few weeks now. We've decided to let people know that we're officially dating."

Did every young woman have to explain it to her own mother like that? Probably not. Mom and Frank didn't live that far away, but far enough that rumors wouldn't just wander over on their own.

"I can't believe this. Do you even *know* what the Cavanagh family is like? What Declan is like?"

"I'm not dating Declan."

Her mother huffed. "Well, I should hope not. The man's pushing sixty. I don't know what Kathryn ever saw in him. I've always wondered why she married him so quickly after

Joe died." Mom raised her eyebrows at Carey. "Please let me know when you've solved that little mystery."

"It's probably none of our business."

"Maybe, maybe not. I was sorry when Joe passed away, of course, but Kathryn had already cut off all contact with me after the divorce. I don't know if she had any idea what it was like living with your father, but Joe and your dad were close once."

"I remember visiting the ranch when I was little. Uncle Joe was kind to Laurel and me."

"I can't believe you're dating a Cavanagh. I'm sure that man's spiteful blood runs through each one of those boys." Mom frowned. "Ryder? Isn't he the youngest? The other two are already married, aren't they?"

Carey braced herself. "Yes, Ryder's the youngest."

"How old is he? Because, if my memory serves me, he was the baby by quite a lot."

"Almost twenty-five."

"You're practically a cradle-robber."

"Um, no. He might be the last born, but he's definitely a grownup." *And how*, but Carey couldn't let herself be diverted with thoughts of his strong arms and passionate kisses. Not in front of her mother.

"I think you're making a mistake, and it seems you know that, too, or you wouldn't have made a special trip to tell me about it. Not when you've practically become a stranger since you moved back to Jewel Lake."

"Ryder's not a mistake, Mom. You're wrong about that. He's sweet and gentle and wonderful. I can see myself falling in love with him and marrying him and having his children. I can see us growing old together. He's nothing like his father."

"Well, you clearly aren't open to hearing my opinions, so

do what you like. Granny Wilson would be turning over in her grave to hear you talk like that about a younger man, and one from such a disagreeable family, besides."

"Now you're sounding like one of Granny's Regency novels. It's different today."

"Not that different," Mom said darkly.

"You'll see when you get to know Ryder. He's making a reservation at The Meating Place for Friday night. Maybe you and Frank could take a little break and join us for dessert?"

Mom pursed her lips as she studied Carey. "Maybe. I'm making no promises."

"Fair enough." Carey pulled her mother into a hug. "Thanks for everything, and maybe I'll see you then."

She turned back toward her car. Had that gone better or worse than she'd expected? It was hard to know. But at least their relationship was out in the open. She'd thought to give Laurel a call while she was in Missoula anyway, but... no. This was enough rejection for one day.

CHAPTER FOURTEEN

Ryder rounded his shiny black truck to open the passenger door for Carey, then took her hand to help her down. After all, even the running boards wouldn't help enough for a lady in heels like hers with their fancy ribbons criss-crossing up her calves. His fingers ached to trace the lacing, but he resisted.

She stood in front of him, a dusky pink dress clinging to her curves and swirling at her knees. Her hair was in an updo with wisps around her face, and she looked up at him, her pink lips parted.

He kissed her lightly, just because he could, then closed the door and beeped the locks. He reached for her hand, but she tucked it behind his elbow more formally. That would be okay. Those heels put her closer to his height. He could kiss her again… no. They had a reservation at her parents' restaurant. He wasn't going to mess this up by acting like a hormonal teen.

"You're beautiful." He squeezed her hand against his side and grinned down at her.

"You mentioned that."

"It bears repeating."

Carey took a deep breath. "Thank you."

"Nervous?"

"Maybe a little. I want everyone to like you as much as I do. And my mom kind of has a thing against your family."

Maybe they should have talked this out in advance, but it was too late now. He held the heavy glass door for Carey and ushered her inside the upscale steakhouse. They'd somehow managed to make bricks and boards look modern with the steel beams arching over the open space. Plenty of large windows enhanced the urban loft ambience.

A young man dressed in black stood behind the hostess stand. "Good evening. Do you have reservations?"

"Yes, for Cavanagh."

The guy checked his tablet and nodded. "Right this way, please."

Ryder rested his hand on the small of Carey's back as they followed the host to a booth with black leather benches tucked against the brick wall. That small contact anchored him in a space that was unlike anything he'd ever been in before. His brothers were more urbane than Ryder had realized, since they talked about this place so casually. He slipped onto the padded bench across from Carey as the host murmured something about their server and hurried away.

"Fancy place," Ryder commented.

Carey glanced around as though seeing it for the first time. "I guess. Frank and Mom just bought it three or four years ago. They've spruced it up some since then."

"They're happy together?"

"They seem to be."

The server appeared with embossed leather menus then recited the evening's specials, including the wine of the day.

"No, thank you." Ryder didn't need anything messing with his judgment tonight. "Just ice water for me. Carey?"

"Same." She cast a fleeting smile at the server. "With lemon, please."

The server retreated, and Ryder looked at Carey. "You're welcome to order a drink if you want. I didn't mean to make the choice for both of us."

She shook her head. "My dad drank too much. It's pretty rare for me to have a glass of wine. I don't want to become like him."

Loaded comment. Ryder was tempted to take the opening to confess his investigation, but not in such a public place, especially one her mother owned. Later. But he knew the disclosure had to come. "Declan doesn't drink. There never alcohol in the house at Rockstead."

"Really? I would have pegged him…"

"My grandfather was an alcoholic, and my father decided young that he would never fall into that trap."

"That's commendable."

"Yes." Ryder leaned on the thick wooden table. "He's not a bad man, really. Just opinionated and brash and angry all the time."

Carey laughed lightly. "How did you grow up so unlike him?"

"Kathryn," he said without hesitation. "And God."

"My aunt is an amazing woman. I've sure liked getting to know her better in the past couple of years."

"Are you ready to order?"

Ryder blinked at the server. "Give us a few minutes?" At

the woman's nod, he smirked at Carey. "I guess we should focus. What's good here? What do you recommend?"

"Hard to go wrong with surf-and-turf."

Ryder wasn't much for seafood, but give him a big slab of meat? Yes, please. But maybe he should expand his horizons. It wasn't like he didn't get plenty of beef at the ranch.

"There's a platter for two, if you like?" Carey pointed out a menu item from the fourth page. "A sampler of prawns, clams, mussels, and crab cakes with twice-baked potatoes and two six-ounce steaks."

Ryder scanned the offering. It came with a smoked salmon paté appetizer and choice of desserts at the other end. "Sure, that looks good. What's your favorite seafood?"

"Dungeness crab. But these crab cakes are good, too."

It was only since hanging out with Carey that he'd begun to wonder how other people lived in other places. The ranch had been his everything. He'd processed Vivienne's desire for college and travel as understandable for someone who'd been shuffled around so much all her life. Someone who didn't know where she belonged. He belonged at Rockstead. No question.

But Carey? She had a good job she seemed to love as a physical therapist. Would she be happy living up at the ranch? Would they build a house down in Cavanaghville like his brothers? Would she want to live in town, and he'd commute up every day? Because he couldn't imagine doing anything else besides wrangling cows and baling hay. It was his life.

What if she didn't want to stay in Jewel Lake? No, that was unthinkable. He could probably survive an occasional vacation elsewhere — although not to Maine — but if she didn't see herself right here in Montana for the rest of her years, he should discover that soon.

Could he move if she asked it of him? Find a different job? Maybe he wasn't too old to go back to school, but with what end goal? He shook his head.

"Deep thoughts?" Carey's warm hand covered his and squeezed.

He managed a laugh. "Overthinking things, as usual."

"I'm good at that, too."

"Oh, yeah?" He turned his hand over so they were palm to palm. His thumb smoothed circles on the side of hers.

Of course, that's when the server reappeared, but Ryder didn't need his hands to place their order. When the woman had nodded and turned to the next table, he pasted a big smile on his face and turned back to Carey. The smile was real. How had he gotten so lucky as to be dating this amazing woman who'd danced in his dreams for nearly two years?

CAREY CHUCKLED at something witty Ryder had said as someone at the end of the table cleared her throat. She glanced up. "Mom! And hi, Frank."

She'd invited them to stop by the table, but she and Ryder had been in their pleasant little bubble for nearly an hour now, and she'd forgotten.

"Hi, Carey." Frank set down the two dessert plates he held and turned to Ryder, stretching out his hand. "Frank Chamberlain, Carey's stepfather."

Ryder half-stood, probably all he could manage within the booth's confines, and shook Frank's hand. "I'm Ryder Cavanagh." He nodded at Carey's mom. "Pleased to meet you both."

"Ellen Chamberlain." Mom assessed Ryder so coolly that it brought a blush to Carey's cheeks.

Carey scooted down the bench. "I see you brought dessert for four. Why don't you have a seat?" She should have warned Ryder, but she honestly hadn't thought Mom would take her up on the offer. Too late now.

Mom set down two more dessert plates and slid in beside Carey. There was an awkward moment while Ryder shuffled over and Frank settled beside him.

"We brought our signature apple and cinnamon creme caramel cakes." Mom distributed the plates. "See? I remembered that chocolate reacts with your rosacea."

"Thank you. These look amazing. Don't you think so, Ryder?" Carey couldn't help pleading with her date. He still looked a bit like a deer caught in the headlights.

"Um, yes. Thank you. Just what I'd already planned to order." He picked up his fork but looked uncertain who should lead.

Carey popped a small bite into her mouth and nearly sagged as the delicious cream cheese layer melted in her mouth. "Mmm. I can see why this is popular."

"It's our top-selling non-chocolate dessert." Frank took a big bite.

"So, Ryder Cavanagh." Mom eyed Ryder. "I would never have seen this coming."

Ryder's fork was halfway to his mouth. Now he set it back on his plate and met Mom's gaze with a smile. "I didn't, either. You've raised an amazing daughter."

Carey dared to breathe.

"She turned out pretty well." Frank winked at her.

"No thanks to her father," Mom grumbled.

Frank covered Mom's hand with his huge one. "Let bygones be bygones. She's good now. We all are."

Ryder shot Frank a curious glance. How Carey wished she could see inside his head.

Mom shook her head. "But a Cavanagh."

"I'm sorry you don't seem to think that's a good thing." Ryder studied Mom. "I'm sure my dad's made a few enemies over the years with his blustering ways, but at the core, he's an honest, good man. He runs one of the biggest ranches in this part of Montana."

"So, what's your background, other than working on your dad's ranch?" Frank glanced sideways. "You know, your plans for the future."

"I'm a cowboy, sir. A rancher. My brothers and I all work for the brand. It's a good, honest life."

Frank shoveled in another bite, the only one of them who had tackled their dessert. He nodded as he wiped his mouth on a napkin. "Any college degree? Any other plans?"

"No, sir. Rockstead Ranch is everything to me. Besides my relationship to God, that is."

Mom leaned forward. "And where does my daughter fit into that?"

Carey cringed, her face flaming as though she'd eaten an entire pan of brownies.

Ryder gave her a reassuring smile before looking back at her mother. "We're still pretty new, so we haven't hammered out what the future might look like for us. But God remains my top priority, no matter what." Now he held Carey's gaze. "And I'm committed to the ranch, as well. But if Carey and I continue, we'll make those decisions together down the trail."

Frank nodded until Mom glowered at him. Then he

scraped his fork across his plate as though surprised there wasn't more of the dessert remaining.

"I'm not convinced God cares all that much." Bitterness soured Mom's voice. "But Carey's on that religious kick, too, so maybe you deserve each other."

"It's not a kick, Mom." Carey nudged her with her shoulder. "God has been my anchor for many years now. I'm not sure how I would have survived without knowing a loving God has plans for my life."

Mom shook her head. "I'm glad you can see the love. Not me. Not ever since your father—"

Frank covered her hand with his, and that seemed to cut off her vitriol.

"I guess divorced parents are another thing Carey and I have in common," Ryder said. "In my case, my mother abandoned us boys to our father, and I've only seen her a couple of times since their split. Carey is lucky to have you in her life."

Carey smiled at him. It was true — the shared background did help them understand each other. And gave them both that much more incentive not to do that to any kids they might ever have. Not that they'd spoken of their *own* kids. Just hypothetical future ones.

"Monica is a piece of work."

Carey shouldn't be surprised her mother knew Ryder's.

"I'm sure Kathryn was a vast improvement, even with all that depression. But I hear she and your father are separated now."

Ryder dipped his head. "They are, but all us kids are praying they'll get back together."

Mom harrumphed. "Sometimes it's best to leave things as they are. Move on." She smiled at Frank, but it didn't quite reach her eyes.

"Has your father contacted you lately?" Frank asked.

Carey hesitated. "Laurel told me he might be coming out to visit soon." She stole a glance at Ryder, since she hadn't told him yet. Her sister had only mentioned it last night on the phone. But why had Ryder stilled so completely? His gaze had narrowed on her, nothing like the sweet smile he usually wore.

Mom muttered something under her breath, but Carey couldn't pick out the words. They probably weren't fit for polite company, anyway.

"You'll meet up with him, then? You don't have to, you know, if you don't want to." Bless Frank for supporting her.

"Probably. I mean, not much could restore the relationship we once might have had, but he *is* my dad, and I haven't seen him in ages."

"Why's he coming now, when he hasn't been for so long?" Ryder's voice had a slight edge to it.

"He told Laurel he had some things he needed to straighten out." She shrugged. "Apparently, he didn't elaborate."

Mom huffed. "As though that man could even figure out what that means. His life is full of twisted lies."

"God can redeem him." Carey wanted to sound confident, but the oddness of Ryder's facial expression shook her a little. What was up with him? "Did you ever meet my dad, Ryder?"

He blinked. "Not that I remember. I was just a little kid when all that would have gone down."

"Yes, you're the youngest, right?" Mom said it as though it were an insult.

Carey should have known Mom wasn't ready to meet any guy Carey might be dating, let alone Ryder.

Frank glanced around the dining room. "We should get back to work, Ellen."

"Yes, we should." Mom surged to her feet. "Carey, don't fall for anything your father says, okay? And call me when you're ready." She gave Ryder a significant look then turned back to Carey.

You mean when I've come to my senses and broken up with Ryder? Thanks a lot for your support, Mom.

Frank guided Mom away from the table. When they'd disappeared into the kitchen, Carey took a deep breath and turned back to Ryder. "Well, that wasn't at all awkward. Sorry."

"You didn't tell me your dad was coming."

Out of that entire conversation, *that* was what he focused on? "I just found out, but it's not like it really matters."

Ryder pushed his half-eaten dessert away. "Ready to head over to the Roxy? The show starts soon."

Carey would never understand men.

CHAPTER FIFTEEN

The music was probably very good. Several of western Montana's most popular bands played, and the audience seemed to be into it. Carey certainly was. She swayed and clapped along, her eyes bright.

But all Ryder could think about was Jason Anderson. He was coming back to straighten a few things out. What kinds of things? Why now? Had he caught wind of Branson's investigation? Would he call Ryder out?

Ryder should never have let things get to this stage. He should have made his decision two years ago that a future with Carey was more important than whatever her dad might — or might not — have done in the vague and distant past.

But there hadn't seemed to be any hints of a relationship with Carey back then. It had only been his youthful infatuation with the best friend of his older sister-in-law. Carey insisted they didn't need to talk about age anymore, but it was hard to forget it completely when he remembered how much angst he'd felt for so long. How much of a kid he'd been.

Yeah, his feelings had matured. He hoped *he* had, too. He'd be twenty-five soon. Not that many decades back, most guys would have been married by now. Fathers, even. These days, a little older was more common. It probably had something to do with much of the population living together before making the big commitment. What was the big hurry if you already had many of the benefits of marriage?

That wasn't Ryder's way, though. Nor Carey's. They hadn't discussed it specifically — talk about an awkward conversation! — but Ryder had seen the mess some of his brothers had made. Nathaniel's comment the other day about his own mistakes resonated with Ryder.

But with Jason Anderson returning, Ryder felt a little like a wild mustang who suddenly discovered he was headed into a funnel toward a high-walled log stockade from which there'd be no escape. He wanted to freak out and buck and bolt.

He *was* freaking out. His gut felt like a block of ice, and even the stifling theater, the throbbing music, the screaming fans, and Carey's shoulder and hip pressed against his did nothing to settle him.

He should have been up front from the beginning. Should have asked her about her dad.

Really? He should never have taken up the investigation to begin with. He couldn't blame it all on Branson, though his buddy had talked about wanting a side project somehow related to his law classes. Ryder had mentioned the bits the family knew — how Jason had tried to use his insurance company to get his hands on his brother's ranch. How, failing that, he'd tried for his brother's wife, who then quickly married Declan. How Jason had disappeared amid rumors of striking the motherlode.

Branson had been intrigued and jumped on the case.

What harm could it do?

Plenty, it turned out. Ryder really needed to talk to his friend. But more than that, he needed to come clean with Carey.

And then... he was going to lose her, wasn't he? That was what the numbness in his gut was telling him. How could she possibly understand, when he couldn't really himself? How could she possibly forgive?

Yeah, there wasn't much love lost between her and her father, but Ryder could understand dysfunctional relationships. He was fully aware of Declan's foibles and faults, but the man had good points, too. He ran a tight ship on the ranch, kept the spread in the black and the guys busy. Treated all six sons fairly. He was even coming around with Vivienne, if a guy looked closely. There was hope for restoration in his marriage to Kathryn, and he wasn't so far gone that God couldn't save him.

Wasn't the same true of Jason Anderson? Yeah, the man had done stupid things, either by impulse or ill intent, but he had to have good qualities, too. Was it really Ryder's place to hound the man to the ground and condemn him?

It wasn't.

Carey jumped to her feet, clapping wildly amid the enthused crowd.

Ryder stared up at her blankly. What was going on? Who'd even sang that last set? He had no idea. All he knew was that he needed out of here. He needed air. He needed space.

He jerked to his feet. "Ready to go?"

She blinked at him. "Now? There are still two more bands to play."

"Yeah. Now."

"Oh. Kay." Confusion clouded her eyes, but she picked up her purse and reached for his hand.

Ryder pretended not to notice as he nudged her toward the aisle. Why had they sat in the middle of a row, anyway? Now they had to excuse themselves over and over as they edged past other festival goers. Finally, they reached the aisle and he picked up speed, steering her in front of him until they reached the exit and — blissfully — the evening air.

Carey pivoted and turned to him, hands on her hips. "Are you okay? What's going on, anyway?"

"I... I just needed air."

"You're claustrophobic?" Her eyebrows shot up.

He wasn't usually. But it almost described the panic he'd felt along with the desperate need to escape, so he nodded. "I'm sorry. I just couldn't take it anymore."

"But... the concert was your idea."

"I know." He clenched his fists at his sides, warring against the desire to gather her close. She wasn't going to want him around when she knew everything, so he might as well get used to it.

He jerked his head toward the parking lot and started for the truck.

How could he explain his reactions tonight? He couldn't. He'd bumble all over himself incoherently. No, he needed a long ride on Champlain. Needed some time to clarify his thoughts and pray.

And to talk sense into Branson.

Then he'd humble himself in front of Carey and throw himself on her mercy. Odds of forgiveness and restoration were very slim. She would see his fixation as juvenile and hurtful — she'd be right on both counts — and that would be the end.

He'd be a wiser cowboy, but would he ever get over her and find someone else to love? Doubtful.

Ryder opened the truck door for her.

Confusion and anger warred on her face as she clambered up with no help from him.

He rounded the vehicle. Now was a fine time to think about loving someone else. Because it drew his attention to the fact that he loved *her*. Not that he knew anything about love. He was just a stupid kid who'd done stupid things and would now get to experience the fallout.

They drove in awkward silence back to Jewel Lake. When he pulled into the apartment parking lot, she jumped out without waiting for him to come around.

"Ryder, when you're ready to explain yourself, you know where to find me." And she slammed the door with enough force to shake the entire sturdy vehicle.

He watched her stomp up the steps in those sexy heels, unlock the outside door, and disappear into the building. Then he released a long breath. He deserved her anger and more.

Oh, God, what was he going to do? Was there any hope of restoration? Because, with everything added together, he'd destroyed any trust they'd built between them. She just didn't know how badly yet... but she would.

CAREY PACED HER APARTMENT. She'd untied and kicked off those stupid shoes but hadn't taken the time to change her clothes. She deserved to be uncomfortable outwardly as well as inwardly.

For the millionth time, she rewound the evening. It had started so promising. The meal had been delicious. Ryder had even fed her a few bites across the table, looking deeply into her eyes with an adorable grin.

It had gone downhill when Mom and Frank joined them. When Mom couldn't stop picking on Ryder for his age and parentage — neither of which the man could help — and then mentioned Dad.

That was the real crux right there. That's when Ryder, already defensive, had pulled back. But... why?

They'd talked before about having divorced parents in common, so it wasn't just Dad's existence. They'd acknowledged the insecurities and abandonment issues that stemmed from having a parent blink out of their lives at a vulnerable age.

She stared out the window. Unlike Kathryn's apartment upstairs, Carey's faced the playground behind the building and not the lake. There was nothing happening out there tonight, just a few lamp posts providing dim little circles of illumination to the swings and slides.

Carey wished she had even that much enlightenment on what had gone down with Ryder tonight. He'd withdrawn so completely, so suddenly, that she'd had no time to react and pull him back before he was locked inside his own head.

Something must have happened. Had he received a text? Surely, she would have noticed. No, his attention had seemed solidly on the conversation, on gently defending himself to Mom. Carey had been so proud of him.

Until he'd shut down.

She raked her mind, trying to pinpoint the exact moment. What had they been talking about specifically? She'd mentioned Dad told Laurel he was coming to visit.

But why would that matter to Ryder? It couldn't. His

estranged mother lived in Jewel Lake now, and he rarely saw her. Never sought her out.

What if the situation were reversed? Monica lived far away and said she was coming to straighten some things out? Would he reject that from his own mother?

Maybe.

But would it put him into such a tailspin? She couldn't imagine it. Ryder was so solid, so unflappable.

And yet something had definitely flapped him tonight.

Carey dropped into her Victorian tub chair and closed her eyes. She could forget that Ryder was nearly four years younger than her... but not when he acted like a moody teen. Then the age difference leaped out at her like a jack-in-the-box with a creepy clown face.

Her phone buzzed with an incoming text, and she surged for it. Ryder already? No. Laurel.

Carey thumbed into her text app and read her sister's message: *Hey, how was your hot date? Mom told me who you're dating!!!! How come you never told me?*

Because... why? She'd told herself it was because their relationship was so new and sweet, and she didn't want it sullied with public speculation. Or was it really because she'd known it wouldn't last? Maybe she'd known that those three-and-a-half years truly did matter, and she'd see why soon enough.

She didn't want to talk to Laurel about it. Not now, when everything was so confusing, but her phone buzzed again. Wow, her sister was nothing if not insistent. But a quick glance revealed the sender this time was Stephanie.

Uh oh. Did Carey even want to know?

The words, *Eli broke up with me*, were followed by half a dozen crying emojis.

Laurel could wait. Carey tapped Stephanie's number. "Oh, hun, I'm so sorry."

"I just can't believe it. I thought he was the one. He's so perfect."

Carey shook her head. Had she been as blind to Ryder's issues as Stephanie had been to Eli's? How could she blame her friend for not seeing this coming when she'd lived in a similar state of denial?

Even now, her mind cried out that it wasn't the same. That things with Ryder really had been perfect until a couple of hours ago. That there'd been no way to foresee this could happen. Yet she'd known about their age difference and the family connections and decided they didn't matter. Maybe Stephanie had rationalized things with Eli in the same way.

"Did he say why?" Dread filled Carey's gut. "Is it because of Harper?"

A newcomer to town, Harper Satterfield was filling in at the church office as Mrs. McDiarmid recuperated from a heart attack. She and Eli would run into each other constantly at work, and the Southern woman was both beautiful and charming.

"He said it's not." Stephanie hiccupped through her tears. "He says he... he never felt about me the way I did about him."

"That's rough." Though would it have been better if Eli said he was dumping Stephanie to be with Harper?

"I just don't know what to *do*!" Stephanie wailed. "My parents are going to be devastated. I don't even know what to tell them."

Carey frowned. "Why will it matter so much to them?"

"I told you. They're sure I'm destined to be a pastor's wife, and Pastor Marshall is already taken. Thankfully."

A laugh sputtered out at the thought of Stephanie with the

grandfatherly, rotund senior pastor. "Oh, girl. That's too much."

Stephanie sighed. "What am I going to do?"

A question Carey was also asking herself. "I don't know. Keep going to work every day, thankful you don't have to see him there?" Same for her. Stephanie worked at the bank, so Eli wouldn't come in any more frequently than Ryder came into the physical therapy clinic.

"And pray Eli realizes what's been in front of him all along and changes his mind?"

Ouch. "Instead, how about praying that God's will be done? You know God cares about you, right? That you're worth far more to Him as Stephanie Simpson, His beloved child, than anything you could bring to Him as Eli's wife."

And *she* was worth more to God as Carey Anderson than anything to do with being Ryder's girlfriend. Her identity was in Christ alone.

"I guess."

"I *know*. And so do you."

Stephanie sighed. "I've tried so hard to do everything my parents wanted. Everything the church teaches. I've been such a good little girl, you know? I helped lead the youth group when I was a teen. I've taught Sunday school and helped in the nursery and led countless studies and groups. I even chaired the missions committee. And it seems to all be for nothing. What does it matter?"

"Don't do anything rash while this is all fresh and new, Steph. Promise me. Pray about it and ask God to really shower His love on you. He *sees* you, my friend. He cares."

"Yeah. I guess. And I guess Harper and I can still be friends, right?"

"Of course." Keep your friends close and your enemies

closer, and all that. Though it was hard to think of Harper as Stephanie's enemy. Was Eli telling the truth about the reason for the breakup, that it wasn't about Harper? But a pastor wouldn't lie about something like that.

"Thanks for calling me, Carey. I needed someone to keep me grounded."

"No problem. That's what friends are for."

"And I'm sorry. You had a big date tonight. Did you have fun?"

"I'll tell you all about it sometime." Sometime in the way distant future. Carey didn't want to heap more angst and emotion into their conversation. Stephanie deserved to be seen and heard without Carey trying to gain sympathy in return.

Besides, she was still trying to figure out what had actually happened. Other than Ryder driving away from her with a scowl instead of a kiss.

Could she find something in her pious advice to Stephanie to apply to herself?

CHAPTER SIXTEEN

Once again, Ryder sat in his truck just around the bend from Cavanaghville, where cell service still existed. He rubbed his forehead, trying to think past the pain in his head, his heart, everywhere. "Bran, this has got to stop."

"Dude. Do you know where your mother is?"

Ryder shook his head to clear it. Not that it helped. "I saw Kathryn minutes ago, babysitting Nat and Ainsley's kids, so they could go out. Why?"

"Not Kathryn. Your *mother*."

Dread filled Ryder's gut. And here he hadn't thought any room remained for more feelings in his body. "You mean Monica. Where is she?"

"In Maine."

"In Maine?" he repeated dully.

"She's at Jason Anderson's seaside cottage. That info barely cost me anything, dude. The next-door neighbor is a busy-body happy to tell all. She's understandably horrified, and she doesn't even know who Monica is."

Ryder straightened in the truck seat and drummed his free hand on the steering wheel. "Why is she there?"

"Ah ha! You don't actually want me to stop looking into things now. They've just taken a most interesting turn."

He'd already lost Carey. Why not indulge his curiosity? But the information sat like he'd swallowed a sixteen-ounce steak without chewing. "You know what, Bran? I don't care what Monica does. I don't care what Jason does. Stop investigating him. I don't want to have to block your number, but I'm going to, if you don't promise me."

Branson scoffed.

Ryder waited one beat. Two. Three.

"You're serious?"

"As serious as life and death."

"I don't get it. We're *this* close—"

"Branson."

"But this is like a soap opera, only real life." His friend coughed. "Not that I've ever watched 'Days of Our Lives' or anything like that."

"Just the fact you know the name of a soap tells me everything I need to know."

Branson's chuckle sounded weak. "Yeah, well, my mom is into them, you know?"

"That has nothing to do with Jason Anderson. Promise me."

"Fine. Whatever. I'd think you'd want to know what your girlfriend's dad is doing. You marry her, and Jason will be your father-in-law."

"We broke up." The words sounded dead. Final. Because they were. Ryder had been such a moron.

"You what? Oh, man. She found out and ditched you?"

"No." Ryder let out a long, slow breath. "She doesn't know

about that, but I can't live with myself. I broke her trust, even though she doesn't know it yet."

"You're not making any sense."

"You know how she's three and a half years older than me? I'm a kid, just a spoiled brat pretending to be a grownup. Playing games with people's lives and reputations. My brothers told me ages ago to let it go, so this is me, accepting adulthood, and letting it go."

Branson laughed harshly. "So now you're calling *me* a kid."

"Didn't say that, man. Not at all. You've had your project, learned more about how the system works. Private investigators can make good money legally. Use your powers for good."

"I still think I'd rather be an attorney."

"Then do that. But, Bran, this investigation on Jason Anderson is officially, completely, irrevocably over. Got it?"

"Yeah, man. I get it." Branson huffed. "Well, your loss."

Ryder thought about that a minute. His brothers had managed just fine without the obsession that had driven Ryder. They'd accepted the ways the chips had fallen and lived their days in the here and now, wrapped up in the loves of their lives and the simple pleasures of working the ranch on horseback.

Why had he been lured by a desire for revenge?

Maybe there was a little of the needy child lurking there still. He'd always been the tail-end, half forgotten by his father and his brothers. Cracking this cold case would have brought him attention. But it wasn't the kind of spotlight he wanted anymore. Now all he wanted was Carey, but he'd let his own pet project ruin what might have been the best thing in his life.

"Okay, well, if that's everything, I'll get out of your hair."

Branson had promised, right? Ryder sighed. "Thanks, buddy. I appreciate you. I do."

"Yeah, okay. Maybe I'll see you around sometime when I'm back home."

"Sure. Look me up." Ryder tapped to end the call and dropped the cell on the passenger seat. He stared out the windshield at the North Star. A steadfast point in the night sky capable of keeping seamen and cowboys alike oriented to everything around them.

God was like the North Star, and Ryder had been busy watching the Big Dipper rotate around it instead of keeping his eye on the one fixed point. He'd been distracted by his attraction to Carey, by his unhealthy fixation on her father, and by his position in his large, dysfunctional family.

All that needed to be set aside. The other constellations — the dippers, Cassiopeia, Orion — would stay in his periphery in their proper seasons, but they shouldn't be his focus.

It was dark right now, but the moon would soon be rising. And morning would dawn at its rightful time.

Who has measured the water in the hollow of his hand and marked off the heavens with a span, enclosed the dust of the earth in a measure and weighed the mountains in scales and the hills in a balance?

That was Isaiah 40:12, a verse he'd learned at Kathryn's knee as a small boy.

And here bitty boy Ryder Cavanagh had been trying to play in the big leagues. Whatever Jason had — or hadn't — done all those years ago was between him and God. God was the one who'd promised vengeance. How did that go, again? Right.

Beloved, never avenge yourselves, but leave it to the wrath of

God, for it is written, "Vengeance is mine, I will repay, says the Lord."

Ryder bent his forehead to the steering wheel. "I'm sorry, Lord. I've completely lost sight of who You are, and who I am. Mostly, I lost sight of who I'm *not*. I'm not in charge. You are."

He'd even thrown that in Dad's face not so long ago, reminding his father that he wasn't the king of the universe, but God was.

Ryder hadn't even seen the hypocrisy at the time. He swallowed hard and looked out the windshield again. Either there were clouds covering the stars now, or his breath had condensed on the cab window, or... or maybe he had tears in his eyes. Either way, he didn't have a clear view of the North Star in the dark night.

But it was there, whether he could see it or not. And God's guiding light was always in his heart, if he only bothered to fix his focus on it.

"Oh, God, I've messed up. I'm sorry. I repent. And I know You will forgive me, that the blood of Jesus covers this wreck and so much more, and I appreciate that so much more than I can say."

He paused a moment, feeling the truth of redemption in his heart. Felt the healing balm of Jesus' love penetrate his soul.

"But, Lord, I've hurt Carey. I don't know what to do about that. I mean, I'll apologize, but will it be enough? It won't be. I know it. I've wrecked the best relationship I've ever had in my life."

The best?

"Besides You, Lord.

There is nothing else that matters.

Ryder knew that. He did. But was it wrong to place value

on a human love, too? Look at his brothers. They had it all, loving wives *and* a strong faith. But it hadn't always been that way.

Adam had tried to manipulate his future, too. Pretended to be engaged to Riley to push Dad into relinquishing Running Creek to him and his brothers. He and Riley had fallen in love for real... but they'd still had to live out their punishment before Dad let them move into Adam's parents' former home.

Travis and Dakota... man, Ryder didn't even want to think about the mess they'd made and the years they'd passed Toby back and forth every weekend while each remained too stubborn and selfish to take the first step toward reconciliation. But God had worked in them, too, and now look at them. Toby adored his baby sister, Penelope. Once Travis had submitted to God, the way had smoothed in front of them.

Then there was Nathaniel, who'd also let his passions overwhelm his good sense. But then Ainsley had disappeared for two years, and came back with a baby, not remembering Nat was Bella's father. Nathaniel had had to woo her all over again, but Bella had always been part of the goal. If Nat could win the same woman twice, maybe Ryder could, too?

Cocky, over-confident Blake. He'd needed a woman to take him down, literally, to make him realize he wasn't God's gift to women. But God had nailed down Blake's attention, partly through Dafne and her little boy, Gavin. Now look at them. They'd been married almost a year, and a more contented husband Ryder had never seen.

And Noah. He might not have messed up as much as some of the rest of them, but he'd tried to control everything he could, too. Probably came from the same root as Ryder's issues. All of the boys had been pulled this way and that through their parents' problems. But Taryn's folks made

Ryder's look benign. She'd run away from her own wedding because of her domineering, greedy father. She and Noah had both had to learn to trust. To realize that God was their rescuer, and they weren't in control.

Ryder wasn't in control, either. Why had he pretended he was?

It was all up to God. It always had been. The difference now? Ryder saw it.

SOMEONE KNOCKED FIRMLY on Carey's apartment door. She raised her head and stared that direction. Whoever that was should have buzzed her intercom and asked to come up. She'd have ignored it, of course. She had yesterday, twice. Because her windows did not face the parking lot, she didn't even know who she'd rejected.

Didn't matter. She wasn't ready to see anyone, not after what happened two nights ago. If it were Ryder, she didn't want to see him. Much.

She wanted answers. But she didn't want to seem eager and then be snubbed again. No matter how she replayed the events of Friday evening, she couldn't make sense of them. Which was probably all on her. Her eyes had been full of stars, her feet had floated above the ground, and she'd been just as giddy as any stupid story's heroine.

And if someone else stood in the corridor, she didn't want to blubber all over them. So, it was best not to talk to anyone. She'd even called in sick to the clinic this morning. She might again tomorrow. It didn't matter. She never used her sick days. Surely heartsick counted.

This time the knock was louder. Sharper.

It might be Ryder. He could have had Kathryn or one of the girls let him into the building. She could peer through the little peephole and see?

But the person might notice that. She didn't want to be seen, not like this. She'd worn her flannel granny nightgown all weekend. Binged on frozen pizza and ice cream. Had she even brushed her hair? She touched her head. Ugh. No, she wasn't taking a chance on that door.

A few seconds later her cell pinged with an incoming text. Relief warred with disappointment to see Ainsley's name on the home screen rather than Ryder's.

Open the door. I know you're in there.

Wow, someone had gotten all bossy.

Should she obey? Text back? Ignore it completely? Carey bit her lip and stared at the screen. Watched the three little dots bounce around.

I'm not going away. In ten minutes, I'm calling your landlord and making my case to get a key. Your aunt will back me up.

Ainsley would do it, too. And that explained how she'd gotten past the locked front door.

Carey shuffled over to the door and opened it a crack, leaving the security chain in place. "Go away. I'm not feeling well."

Ainsley's face appeared in the crack, and her eyes widened. "Whoa, girl, you look terrible. Open up."

"No."

"Do it."

Did Carey really want to cut off every single person in her life? Then she might as well take Laurel up on her hare-brained plan for them both to move out of state. Except she'd been ignoring her sister's texts and calls, too.

She slid the chain out of its groove and stepped back. "Fine. Suit yourself."

Ainsley shut the door behind her and put both hands on her hips as she assessed Carey. "Jeepers, girl. You're a mess."

Carey slumped into the nest of blankets she'd made on the sofa. Say what you will, those Victorian-era sofas weren't that comfortable without a lot of help.

Ainsley perched in the tub chair across from her. "What happened?"

"Don't your children need you?"

"I left the girls with Kathryn upstairs. She's thrilled to have them, and she's worried about you. I even left a bottle of expressed milk with her for Oakley, so I'm in no hurry to get back there. Talk to me."

"Ryder and I broke up."

"I figured it was something like that. He looks just as awful as you do."

Yay. Two miserable people. Get out the party hats and celebrate.

"You might as well start from the beginning, because I already told you I have all night."

Carey stared at Ainsley. "It won't make any difference, but sure. We had dinner at Mom and Frank's restaurant Friday night. I'd told my mom I was coming in with Ryder. I knew she might have something to say about it, but I didn't expect her to be quite as condescending as she was. I just… I just figured she loved me and trusted me enough to make my own decisions, you know?"

Ainsley snorted. "You're talking to the woman whose mother took advantage of my traumatic brain injury and the resultant amnesia and managed to break Nathaniel and me up for nearly two years."

Right. Carey didn't have a corner on miserable parents. Even though Carey's own dad was a jerk, at least she knew who he was. "Mom managed to make what had been a pleasant dinner into something awkward. Then she started whining about my father. I mean, I know he's not that great, right? But she said he was coming to visit."

Ainsley quirked her eyebrows. "And then?"

"Ryder got kind of quiet. We went over to the Roxy, and I could see he wasn't really into the festival, but I thought it was pretty cool. Some of my favorite bands. Then all of a sudden, he decided he was done, and it was time to come home. It wasn't even over yet."

"Oh, no…"

"Oh, yes. I had no idea what his problem was. I honestly still don't. He hardly said a word all the way back to Jewel Lake. Whatever got stuck in his craw, he wasn't talking about it. So, at the apartment, I jumped out of the truck and told him he knew how to find me if he ever wanted to."

"And has he?"

"Does it look like it?" Carey let out a bitter laugh.

"Would you let him say his piece if he did?"

She sighed. "The longer it takes, the more I think not. I might look for a job in California."

"Two more stubborn people…" Ainsley muttered.

"Do you know what his problem is? Because if you do, enlighten me, please." Carey crossed her arms over her flannel-covered chest.

Ainsley studied her. "Will you promise me one thing?"

"I'm not sure."

"Don't give up on him. He's a good kid…" She winced.

"See? That's what I mean. No one takes him seriously. He's not a kid. He's almost twenty-five!"

"Yeah. I know. Just… there's some stuff. I don't know what all, but I know there's a trigger in there somewhere about irresponsible parents. Please, when he comes to his senses and comes crawling back to apologize, will you let him talk?"

"Maybe. I don't know. I hate getting jerked around like this."

"I get that. And I'm not excusing him, just explaining from what I know of him and all of the brothers. Their parental situation puts the 'dys' in dysfunctional just as much as yours and mine did. But I know that with a little time and God's help, Ryder can shed that. His brothers did. He will, too."

CHAPTER SEVENTEEN

Ryder! I haven't seen you in ages."

He stood at the gate of Kathryn's garden between the house and the creek. It hadn't been tended much in the past couple of years since she'd taken the girls and moved to town, but it was still filled with profuse blooms.

"I've been... busy."

"Too busy for your mama?" She angled her head and grinned at him.

A tiny bit of his cold heart melted. "Can we talk?"

"Sure. Out here?" She beckoned at the garden bench near the pond.

He glanced at the deck above. Was his father in the house? Because he didn't wish to be overheard.

"Or inside." Kathryn led the way to the French doors that opened into what had been her basement refuge when her marriage to Dad had first splattered on the rocks.

Ryder remembered his brothers renovating the space into a nice little apartment for her with a bedroom, a bathroom, and a living room that doubled as a school room for him and the twins. He hadn't been old enough to be much help, but he'd toted tools and helped where his awkward teenage self had been able to.

There wasn't much in the space now. Noah and Nathaniel had moved her furniture to the apartment in town two years ago when Dad had become even more of a moron than he'd been before. When his brief affair with Ainsley and Vivienne's mom had come to light, along with the fact that he was Viv's father.

That had been the breaking point for Dad and Kathryn. Not because Kathryn couldn't accept his past. After all, they hadn't been married at the time of Vivienne's conception. More because Dad was bent on continuing to pretend his other daughter didn't exist, and Mom chose to open her arms wide to the messed-up teen.

Things had changed some. Dad had let Viv move to the ranch a couple of months ago and take on the stablehand job. She lived in one of the bunkhouse cabins now and ate her meals with Dad and Ryder. Sometimes Dad even talked to her. Mostly about the horses and cows, but still. It was something. It was civil.

Kathryn settled on the floor with her back to the wall and patted the spot next to her. "Talk to me, Ry."

He dropped down beside her and picked at the carpet. It had seen better days.

So had he.

Ryder glanced at his stepmother. She looked at peace, the lines in her face not as deep as they'd been while she still lived with Dad. Her shoulder length blond hair, tinged with gray, had been pulled into a messy ponytail. "I screwed up."

She nodded. "You're human, I see."

"No. I mean I *really* screwed up."

"Tell me."

"Carey… she's amazing. You probably know that. I don't know what she ever saw in me."

"Ryder. Don't cut yourself short."

"I'm serious." He shook his head and tugged at the carpet again. "She's an incredible woman, and I'm just a kid."

"Pfft."

Ryder blinked at his stepmom. "Have you forgotten how much younger I am?"

"Have you forgotten that it doesn't matter? Honestly, Ryder. Quit flogging that dead horse. You and Carey have been dating for what, a month?"

"Until—"

"A month?"

He sighed. Nodded.

"You are not a child. We all do stupid things, but you can't keep blaming youth for your humanity. You'll still be doing stupid things when you're thirty. Fifty. Eighty."

"If that's supposed to be comforting, you missed the mark."

"I'm not trying to comfort you. I'm calling your age out as an excuse. Cut that mindset loose and man up to whatever the problem between you is. I'm guessing you are talking to me because things are not quite as perfect as you imagined they would be."

Ryder scratched his head. Okay, so if he let that go — truly let it go — then what was left? He'd used their family connections as another excuse for a long time, but he'd already put that to rest. What now?

"You know Branson—"

"I thought you were calling him off."

"I did." He glanced at Kathryn. "The last thing he told me is that my mother is in Maine with Carey's dad."

Kathryn rolled her eyes. "Doesn't that just figure? I knew they had a fling back eighteen, twenty years ago, but—"

"They *what?*" And why was he always the last to know?

"Ed kicked her out last summer. It's why she showed up at Blake and Dafne's wedding with excess alcohol in her system. That poor woman."

"Wait. You feel *sorry* for my mother?"

"Ryder, she doesn't know the Lord. She's trying so hard to figure life out, but she refuses to look to the One who can give her purpose. Of *course*, I feel sorry for her."

"You're incredible. I don't know how you can be so open, so forgiving." Man, all Ryder wanted to do was hold grudges. He should have been paying more attention to Kathryn's mindset all along.

Her hand rested on his knee. "It's taken me a while to get here, Ryder. You figure people shouldn't botch up so much when they're adults. Believe me, age has nothing to do with it. Learning to trust the Lord is a process that takes our entire lives. When we mess up — and we will — then we humble ourselves, ask forgiveness, and move forward."

Ryder stared at his stepmom's hand. "You're wearing your wedding ring."

"I've never taken it off."

"I don't know why you've held out hope."

"Because God is in the business of cleaning up those messes we're talking about."

"Yeah, but Dad…"

"Don't you see the changes in him?"

Ryder thought about it. "Maybe?" Dad hovered a little less.

Wasn't as rude at meals. There hadn't been an explosion of foul language in quite a while, actually.

"I can see it," Kathryn said quietly. "And before you accuse me of wearing rose-tinted glasses, the counselor we've been meeting with in Missoula is very hopeful, too. Your father harbors guilt for his brother's death. You've heard the story of how Callum was swept away in a flash flood while herding cattle. The thing is, your dad sent him into that draw. He didn't know there'd be a flood, of course. Declan just wanted Callum to do all the hard work while he lorded it over his younger brother."

That was a bit more to the story than Ryder had heard before. And maybe it explained some things about Dad.

"The grief killed your grandmother. Your grandfather — Patrick — blamed Declan for all of it, laying on even more guilt. He'd always favored the younger boy, or at least it seemed like it to Declan. Patrick was an alcoholic. He drank even more after his wife and son passed."

"How old was Dad?"

"Sixteen. Callum was thirteen."

Ryder heaved out a breath. "That's… heavy."

"He never spoke of it before, but it's all come out in counseling. Why he holds the reins so tightly and has trouble letting anyone in."

"I never knew."

Kathryn's head tilted back against the wall. "I didn't, either."

"He couldn't have been that nasty and bitter when he courted you."

"We're not here to talk about your dad and me, are we?"

Ryder shook his head. "No. But it maybe helps."

"What happened with Carey?"

"Has she told you?"

"Not a thing. Ainsley dropped off the girls with me last night while she went in and talked to Carey, but she didn't tell me anything afterward. It's none of my business."

Ryder had nearly worked a tuft of carpet completely loose. "First, Carey's mother thinks I'm just a kid."

"How do you prove you're not?"

He squinted at Kathryn. "What do you mean?"

"The number is what the number is, and the only cure for that is time. But maturity is not the same thing."

Had he acted maturely? Not the way he'd pushed Carey out of the Roxy and then refused to talk to her. He heaved another sigh. "The only way to prove I'm not a kid is to act like an adult."

"Bingo."

He digested that for a moment. Carey made him feel like a man. She told him their age difference didn't matter to her. So why did it bug him when her mom labored the fact? It had put him on edge, but the real clincher had been the news that Jason was coming back to town. And he hadn't even known how it linked to his own mother at that time.

"What's the other thing? You said that was the first." Kathryn glanced over.

"I never should have started Branson after Jason."

"Truth."

"But I did."

"And Carey found out?"

"Not that I know of."

Kathryn elbowed his side. "Don't make me drag every word out of you."

"I got so focused on following Jason's trail, watching for him to mess up, that I didn't think how it would affect her. Or how it was affecting my own spiritual life. It was an obsession."

"You know why Jesus came, right?"

He angled a look at his stepmom. "To seek and to save that which was lost."

"To restore broken relationships. Between God and humanity. Between humanity and creation. And between one broken human being and the next. You're not the first person to take their eyes off Jesus, Ryder. We all do. What matters is what we do when we realize it."

He nodded slowly.

How could he prove he was a mature man? By humbling himself, coming clean with Carey, and asking for her forgiveness.

After he'd done the same with God.

IT SEEMED Ainsley hadn't run back to Ryder with a report. Carey would have killed her best friend if she had. But, on the other hand, someone needed to break this impasse. Or else, she needed to move to California. Was Laurel still interested?

Carey still hadn't answered her sister's text from Friday night, let alone the ones from subsequent days.

She really couldn't call in sick another day. Her worried boss insisted she go to the walk-in clinic soon. This was nothing a doctor could cure.

Laurel had phoned. Not five minutes later, her cell rang again. Fine. Whatever. She tapped to accept.

"Girl, I don't know what's going on with you, but you've got half an hour to get down to the Golden Grill, so move it."

"I don't want—"

"Do I sound like someone who cares?"

No, her sister did not. Carey's stomach chose that moment to remind her she'd been subsisting on junk for four days now. A real meal did sound appealing. The diner made a mean Reuben on rye.

"Caroline! Do you hear me?"

"I hear you."

"It's six o'clock. I'll meet you just outside at six-thirty. Don't stand me up."

It was easier to acquiesce than to argue. "Okay."

Carey took a quick shower, but there wasn't time for additional selfcare. She finger-braided her wet hair into one plait and dabbed on a little blush. There wasn't much she could do about the bags under her eyes without a lot more attention. Besides, what did it matter? Laurel had seen her at her worst many times.

The good people at the Golden Grill might not have, but whatever. Their impressions of her wouldn't matter after she moved away, anyway. She slid a sundress over her head and kicked aside the stupid shoes she'd worn Friday in favor of low, flat sandals. She was down to five minutes when she hurried out to her car.

Downtown, she took a deep breath in her angle parking space facing the park and the lake beyond. Something about the greens and blues anchored her. "Lord? Please give me wisdom for my future."

Carey pushed the car door open. She'd talk to Laurel about California tonight. It was nearly the end of June. She could give notice on her apartment right quick.

She turned toward the Golden Grill across the street and shaded her eyes with her hand. Who was Laurel talking to?

That girl never met a stranger. Here she was, a town away from where she lived, and—

Wait. That was Dad. Dad and a woman? Carey was going to kill her sister.

But they'd spotted her now. All three turned to watch her cross the street. She'd be lucky if she didn't trip over her own two feet and get run over by that oncoming Jeep.

Somehow, she made it to the other side, and Laurel grabbed her arm in a pincher grip. "Hey, good to see you, sis! Surprise!"

Carey tried to shake her sister's hand away, but Laurel didn't let go.

"Carey." Dad stepped forward and wrapped his arms around her.

Once she would have given anything for his attention. Today, she didn't want it. Besides, he smelled like alcohol and cheap perfume.

"Hi, Dad." She disengaged and took another look at the overly made-up middle-aged woman. Wait. She'd seen that woman before, last year at Dafne and Blake's wedding. That was Monica Cavanagh, or whatever her last name was now. She'd married some other poor schmuck after divorcing Declan, hadn't she? But that was a long time ago. Obviously her second husband was also in her rear-view mirror or she wouldn't be hanging out with Dad.

Dad put his arm around the woman's shoulder and smiled at Carey. "I'd like you to meet my girlfriend, Monica. Nika, this is my younger daughter, Carey."

"Pleased to meet you." Carey nearly choked on the words.

"Likewise." The woman purred like a kitten. Or like a tiger. Carey wasn't sure which.

"Great!" Laurel's gaze bounced between them. "Let's get some dinner. Dad's buying."

Still holding her wrist, Laurel dragged Carey into the diner. With Dad's bulky form behind them — to say nothing of Monica — Carey didn't have a hope of escape.

And Ryder thought his family was dysfunctional. Oh, it was, and now it was overlapping into Carey's.

Laurel pushed Carey into a booth, with Monica and Dad across from them.

Estelle Mulligan's face was alive with curiosity as she dropped off menus and took their drink orders. "Monica Germaine! I haven't seen you for a while. Where've you been?"

"Oh, out in Maine. Jason here has an adorable little cottage on the seashore, so we've been all cozied up out there."

"Oooh! How'd you meet each other?"

Dad laughed. "Come on, Estelle, don't tell me you've forgotten me. Jason Anderson. I used to run that insurance office just down the block, remember?"

Estelle's mouth opened and closed as she assessed him.

Carey wanted nothing more than to sink under the table, through the floor, through the entire planet. But that wasn't going to happen.

Monica smirked at Estelle. "Jason and I go way back. And when we discovered we were both free again, we just picked right up where we left off."

Estelle looked between them then glanced at Carey and her sister. "Well, isn't that interesting. I'll leave you for a few minutes and come back to take your order."

"That woman." Monica waved a dismissive hand at Estelle's back. "She has to know just everything. Word will be out all over town in no time flat."

Somehow, Carey figured Monica wouldn't mind if it was. The woman seemed to like being at the center of attention, stirring up trouble.

"You girls should come visit us at the cottage sometime." Monica's voice still seemed too loud, too strident.

"Oh, I'd love to!"

Yeah, Laurel might say that, but not Carey. No way was she going to spend any more time than she had to watching Ryder's sleazy mother run her hands all over Dad, like she was doing now. The woman was nowhere near as classy as Aunt Kathryn.

Carey focused on her father. "Dad, I was surprised when Laurel told me you were coming to visit."

Dad gave her an aw-shucks grin. "I hadn't been back here in a long time, but when Nika and I hooked up, we realized we both had some loose ends that needed taking care of in Jewel Lake."

Loose ends? Now his daughters were nothing more than loose ends?

Monica beamed. "So here we are!"

Did Ryder know his mother was back in town? Too bad she and Ryder weren't speaking to each other, or she'd let him know.

Maybe she should, anyway.

CHAPTER EIGHTEEN

Whatever Kathryn Cavanagh had learned in her life, one thing had become clear: a woman needed to meet her challenges head on.

She hadn't learned that when Joe was ill. She'd just hoped and prayed that God would cure him. Not that faith was a bad thing. Not at all. But in trying to hold the boys and the ranch and her job together, maybe she'd failed Joe. He'd wanted to talk to her about her future after his passing, and she'd pretended he wasn't going to die.

He'd died anyway, and she never found out what he'd meant to tell her.

Maybe he'd been trying to warn her about his brother, Jason. Who knew? But she'd been grieving Joe's death and pushing away Jason's inappropriate advances at the same time. She'd tried to tell Jason no, but then he'd cornered her and kissed her before she'd managed to get away.

Jason was nothing like Joe. And he hadn't been trying to comfort her like a brother. Not even a little bit.

So, when Declan had galloped into her life like a knight in shining armor, wielding his sword, she was only grateful. He made her feel safe. He vanquished Jason and swept her into his fairy tale.

Kathryn had not asked all the right questions, especially the ones about his personal faith. She knew his boys were in church every week, but he had a series of excuses about why he hadn't been able to make it himself any given week.

And once again, she'd put her blinders on. His offer of marriage sounded like security. His three motherless boys needed her. Her three boys needed a father figure — someone who was definitely not their uncle Jason.

She couldn't completely regret any of it. They'd had a few decent years. Their twin daughters were a delight. Or, at least, they had been before turning into hormonal, headstrong teens.

Kathryn had withdrawn again. She'd needed a refuge in the storm. Yes, she'd clung to the Lord, but she'd let her gaze linger on the waves. She and the apostle Peter went way back. He'd blustered along, too, talking bravely and then falling, over and over, just like she did.

Peter had come through it stronger than ever.

Kathryn would, too, because she was done cowering. She'd left Declan two years back, something she'd sworn she'd never do. Marriage was for keeps. Just because she'd made a hasty decision after Joe's death didn't mean she could walk away from her husband and their accumulative sons and daughters.

And that's why she'd checked to see if Monica's cell phone number was the same as it had been after Blake and Dafne's wedding, when Kathryn had given Declan's boys' inebriated mother a ride home. She'd found out then that Monica's husband, Ed, had kicked her out when he'd discovered her sexting with another man.

It took no imagination to figure out the other man was Jason. Estelle Mulligan's call about seeing them together with Carey and Laurel at the Golden Grill a couple of nights ago confirmed Kathryn's dormant suspicions. Not that she approved of the woman's gossiping ways, but she hadn't been able to cut Estelle off before she'd spilled all.

Maybe Kathryn had needed the information.

She looked around the apartment. She still couldn't believe Vivienne had moved up to Rockstead and was working for her father. And the twins were starting their Senior year soon. They were out at youth group tonight.

What they didn't know was that their dad often spent Friday evenings at the apartment. At their counselor's suggestion, they spent a bit of time talking through assigned questions before letting their conversation roam. Sometimes they played a game of cards.

In fact, in the past few months, Kathryn and her husband had spent more time simply talking than they'd done in their entire marriage.

He'd be here any minute.

She smoothed her ruffle-hemmed T-shirt over her jeans and glanced in the mirror one more time. She was fine. The apartment was fine. He'd been here before. It didn't matter. But tonight, it wasn't just Declan coming.

Kathryn shoved the thought aside and sent another prayer heavenward. She'd prayed so much the past couple of days, begging the Lord to give her wisdom. Then to give her courage. God knew she'd lacked both plenty of times.

Why didn't the buzzer buzz? She paced to the living room

window and looked down into the parking lot just as Declan's big black truck turned in. He jumped out, and Kathryn's heart warmed.

She hadn't been in love with him when she married him. And, for years, she'd feared and maybe even hated him. Not anymore. Now the sight of his lean body, clad in newish blue jeans and a denim shirt, his face obscured from above by his brown Stetson, sent pleasurable shivers up her spine.

They were so close to getting back together. The counselor warned them to take each step in order, no rushing, no skipping.

It was hard.

A red convertible squealed into the lot.

Declan turned.

No. They weren't supposed to arrive for another fifteen or twenty minutes. Not until Declan was safely upstairs.

Monica waved at Declan as the car engine died. She sashayed out of that car toward her ex.

Kathryn froze for just a second, but no. She was needed down there before everything backfired on her. She'd thought the four of them needed to sit down, have an open discussion, clear up some baggage, so that she and Declan could both let go of the past.

She whirled and dashed to the door. She careened down the three flights of stairs, through the lobby, and out into the July evening just in time to see Declan pull back his fist. Jason's smirking face seemed a likely target.

Kathryn skidded to a stop beside Declan, her hand on his arm. "Wow, you all ran into each other out here. Why not come upstairs? I've got a pot of tea on and some cookies baked."

Jason's gaze narrowed on hers. "Still at it, Kathryn?"

"I'm not sure what you mean."

"The talking's over."

What? "But I invited you, and you're here." Why not, if not to sort things out?

"You're so naive." Monica must be wearing all the makeup the pharmacy downtown had for sale. "If you're worried I want *him* back"— her chin poked toward Declan —"you're sadly mistaken. You can have him."

"I wasn't — I didn't think that." More to the point, Declan would never accept Monica back, even if he were divorced from Kathryn, which he wasn't. Not that he was a saint, but he was making progress.

"And you've clearly made your choice." Jason's eyes were hard. "I offered you everything—"

That fired up her temper. "What you wanted was *me* to offer *you* everything your brother had worked for. That's not how it goes."

"There's more than one way, Kathryn."

Monica clung to Jason's arm as her eyes flung fiery darts at Declan. "Ain't that the truth."

What were they getting at?

"You dumped me without a backward glance." Monica glowered at her ex.

Declan tensed. Would Monica be his new target? Then he took a deep breath and relaxed slightly. "You're the one who walked out and didn't show your face for years. You left the boys behind, your own flesh and blood. You sent the divorce papers. Don't blame me for not fighting to keep you."

"If you'd loved me…" Monica batted her eyelashes.

The nerve.

Declan laughed harshly. "Don't start. Neither of us had a

clue what love was." His hand found Kathryn's and gripped so tightly her fingers felt like they might fall off.

But the pressure grounded her. And, for once, Declan didn't rise to the bait and launch a tirade. He might not realize how far he'd come, but Kathryn could see it.

If only tonight didn't ruin everything.

Declan's dark gaze fixed on Jason's. "What are you doing here?"

"Your *wife* invited us. Or is she just another ex to you?" Jason eyed their joined hands. "I've heard about your separation."

"If you think she'd go with you now when she wouldn't nineteen years ago, you're dumber than you look."

Anger flared in Jason's eyes. "I don't need Kathryn. I have Monica."

Declan shrugged one shoulder. "Go for it."

"Oh, I already have. We've been together for over a year now."

"Then why are you back here?" Declan asked the question Kathryn was dying to know the answer to.

"Loose ends." Jason's eyes hardened.

Monica tittered.

This was not going well, but at least the men weren't brawling on the parking lot pavement. That was good. Right?

Kathryn broke the silence. "I'm glad you're visiting for the girls' sake. I know Carey and Laurel have both missed having their dad in their lives."

Monica rolled her eyes.

A flare of anger spiked in Kathryn. "As your boys have missed their mother."

"How could they, when they have perfect you?"

"I'm not perfect." So very far from it.

"It was so nice of you to snatch my man before I had a chance to reconsider."

Declan snorted. "You'd been gone two years, Monica."

"Long enough for you to have a little fling with Brenda Johnson and hide the fact you had another kid."

Declan lunged toward Monica, but she stepped behind Jason, laughing.

The two men stood chest to chest, staring into each other's eyes. Jason had a couple of inches on Declan and probably fifty pounds, but Kathryn would put her wager on Declan. Her husband was strong and wiry from working hard on the ranch his entire life.

"I could take you if I wanted to." Declan's voice was low, his eyes hard.

Jason stared back. "Try it. You'll be in jail for assault."

"You're not worth the trouble. You're scum. Get out of Montana and don't bother coming back." Declan shifted his gaze to Monica over Jason's shoulder. "You, too." He pivoted and walked away.

Kathryn dodged out of his way, or he would have run into her. She couldn't have been more proud of her husband.

"Come on, Kathryn. I'd like some of that tea." He held out his hand.

She took it but glanced back at the other couple. What should she say? It was nice to see you? Maybe some other time for tea? Have a nice trip back to Maine? "Goodbye."

Declan unlocked the building door and escorted her inside. When they got up to the apartment, she looked out the window to see the convertible speeding down the street.

Declan stood just inside Kathryn's apartment, his hands wedged firmly in his jeans pockets. If he didn't, he'd either shake her or haul her tight against his chest. The jury was out which way it would go.

She uttered a deep sigh as she turned back into the room. "They've left."

"Good. They should never have been here." And Kathryn had been the one to invite them. "What on earth were you thinking?"

Kathryn crossed her arms over her light blue top, and her brown eyes flashed at him. "Closure. That's what I was thinking."

"Never thought to warn a guy?"

"You wouldn't have come."

"Darn right I wouldn't have." He stared at her.

She lifted her chin and met his gaze.

Oh, how he loved this woman. Loved her fire. He'd tried his hardest not to. Tried to block any touchy-feely stuff from getting past his skin and into his soul. He'd even tried to keep her in her place just so he wouldn't have to admit to feelings.

Loser.

But she was still here. Still kind. Still hopeful.

Still wearing his ring.

Declan let out a long breath. "How do you do it?"

Confusion clouded Kathryn's eyes. "Do what?"

"You just keep on trusting for the best. It's not realistic. The world is a nasty place, full of angry, hurting people. You have to protect yourself better."

Her eyebrows tipped up.

He huffed. "Okay, I'm an angry, hurting person. And you keep letting me back in."

"I love you, Declan."

"Why?" He couldn't have stopped the word if he'd tried.

She hesitated, and he hardened his heart. Again. Of course, she couldn't answer that. He was unlovable. He'd managed to push Monica away. He'd never tried to keep Brenda close. But Kathryn? No matter how badly he treated her, she still figured she loved him?

"Why?" he repeated.

"Because... I see *you*, the man hidden behind the gruff exterior. I see the man whose sense of justice is sharper than nearly anyone else's. I see the man who works hard, is honorable—"

Declan scoffed, but it didn't slow her words.

"—I see the man who works his sons hard, but no harder than he works himself. I see the man who took in his heart-broken wife's three boys and treated them as his own, who insisted on adopting them and giving them his surname, if only to protect them from their money-grubbing uncle. I see the man who dangled two little girls on his knees but didn't know what to do with their moods as they grew. I see the man who encouraged his wife to build a garden, a sanctuary. I see a man..."

When had she crossed the room? Because now she stood within arms' reach, those passionate eyes searching his, the scent of her floral perfume flooding his senses.

He fisted his hands in his pockets. Otherwise, he'd crush her against him, but it wasn't time for that. Still... maybe the time was coming? He could only pray it was.

Pray?

Declan Cavanagh didn't pray. At least, he hadn't in the past. Not much, anyway. There'd been a time or two over the years when he'd begged God to slap a few stupid people upside the head. Monica, for instance.

But that wasn't the kind of prayers Kathryn offered to God. She prayed God's blessing on her enemies.

He snorted a laugh. She invited her enemies for tea and cookies and expected everyone to be friends by the end of the evening.

She tilted her head. "What's so funny?"

"I don't know what to make of you."

"I told you what I see in you." Her voice was soft and low. "What do you see in me?"

"I see someone whose capacity for forgiveness knows no bounds."

"You're confusing me with Jesus."

Once he would have scoffed at her religious talk, but not anymore. Not after watching her in action for nearly two decades. Yeah, he'd managed to push her down into depression, but she'd sprung back. She'd moved out, sure, but she hadn't given up on him.

Kathryn still loved him.

He was undeserving.

She'd told him — the boys had told him — that's how God was, too. Always loving, always holding out hope and love and forgiveness. That God would forgive him for everything if he only asked.

That capacity for love was beyond anything Declan could imagine. Of course, his imagination wasn't that well-honed. He was a practical man who'd had to accept the hardships of life early. Dad's alcoholism. Mom's favoritism of her younger son. His own blame in Callum's death.

Nobody had handed out gold stars to young Declan. Who could blame him for trusting no one but himself?

It was a bitter pill to be fifty-eight years old, only to

discover that the one he'd put his trust in had totally, completely, let him down.

And yet — somehow — his wife still loved him. And God did, too.

A man couldn't just pivot at his age, though. Could he?

CHAPTER NINETEEN

M y dad's been in town all week." Growling, Carey paced Ainsley's living room. "I can't believe he's hooked up with Monica."

Ainsley sat curled up on the corner of the couch, holding the baby, watching her. Nathaniel had taken one look at Carey's stormy face when she knocked on the door then scooped up Bella and said something about Noah needing his help *right now.*

Yeah. She'd probably scared Ryder off that completely, too.

"It sounds like they're two of a kind."

Carey stopped in front of Ainsley. "You know what my mother said?"

"Tell me."

"That Monica was one of the women Dad had an affair with around the time of their divorce. *One* of the women."

"That's got to hurt."

Carey stared at her friend. Right. Ainsley's mother had lived with an entire procession of men. Ainsley didn't even know who her father was. Nothing much Carey could say about her dad would be worse than Ainsley's experience. "I'm sorry."

Ainsley angled her head and raised her eyebrows. "For?"

"For going on and on about my woes when you've dealt with so much worse."

"I don't think it's a competition. Plus, it doesn't negate the hurt you're feeling now. Right on the top of that whole thing with Ryder."

Carey's shoulders sagged. "Is it 'on top of,' or is it all part of the same thing?"

"Meaning?"

"Are all men so unpredictable and only out for themselves?"

Ainsley laughed. "No."

"Of course, you'd protect Nathaniel. You're still in the honeymoon phase."

"Oh, girl, the honeymoon is well over. There's been a lot of stuff."

"You never told me."

"Why would I? Nat and I are a team. We need to work through our own issues, not talk to outside parties who have no skin in the game."

Carey flinched. That hit close to home.

Ainsley laid the sleeping baby on the sofa then rose and reached for Carey.

No. Carey was in no mood for conciliatory hugs.

Ainsley hands dropped to her sides. She angled her head and studied Carey. "If that rejection is for being left out of my marriage to Nathaniel, that's just weird."

"No." Carey held herself stiff. "It's because I was trying to work through things on my own, but you're the one who bulldozed down my door and made me talk. Now you're telling me your stuff isn't any of my business."

Ainsley shook her head. "There's a big difference."

"Oh?" Carey pinned her friend with a glare.

"There is. This stuff with your dad and Monica is bigger than you and Ryder. It's not a private matter between two people who've pledged their lives to each other. And… you and Ryder haven't done that. You haven't irrevocably trusted each other with everything."

"What's that supposed to mean? I trusted him."

"Uh huh."

"Unless you mean he didn't trust me. Because that's more likely."

Ainsley's eyebrows shot up. "How so?"

"There were a few times he seemed about to say something to me but then said it didn't matter. Or something like that. Maybe that was him not trusting me."

"You know what? You guys need to talk."

Carey stared at Ainsley. "Do you know what he wasn't saying?"

"Jeepers, girl. I'm sure he said a lot of things. Everything he didn't say? Are things he didn't say."

"That's not what I mean. You know something."

"Has Ryder tried to contact you?"

"Not for the first few days."

"It's been a week now. So, when did he start?"

"He's texted a few times asking to talk. He phoned once and left a message."

"And you're ignoring him."

Carey glared.

Ainsley tossed her hands in the air. "You come here complaining about how things are with Ryder, and you don't reply when he reaches out? I've got no advice for you. Talk to the guy."

"I believe I was talking about my father." Carey bit out the words. "It's you who brought up Ryder."

"Forgiveness is a thing. You can't just wait for someone to grovel an appropriate amount before relenting and agreeing to let something go. That's not forgiveness. That's being prideful and superior."

Carey didn't want to forgive her dad. He wasn't even apologetic. He'd been all about rubbing her face in his relationship with Monica the other night. No hint of remorse for anything he'd done to his wife or daughters. What kind of loose ends had he been talking about, anyway, if not for that?

She'd missed something.

"My friend, my mother died with this whole thing unresolved between us. Do you remember what she did to me?"

Carey refocused on Ainsley.

"She took total advantage of my traumatic brain injury and the fact that I'd forgotten Nathaniel. She led me to believe that I'd been raped, or it had been a one-night stand, even though I *now* remember telling her about Nathaniel. My mother went to her grave, knowing she was going to die, without apologizing for that. Also, without telling Viv who her father was."

"Your mother was awful." Worse than Carey's dad? Yeah, Ainsley got the prize.

"I forgave her, Carey, even though she never once asked me to."

Carey slumped into a chair. "I don't know how you could do that."

"Bitterness wasn't solving anything. It was eating my own soul instead."

She closed her eyes and rubbed her temples. Bitterness really didn't alleviate the problem, but the thought of telling Dad she forgave him when he obviously had few, if any, regrets grated on her like nails on a chalkboard. Was it easier for Ainsley to forgive because her mother no longer had the power to hurt her in new ways?

Maybe.

Maybe not.

The door flung open and crashed against the wall. Carey whirled to see what was going on only to see Nathaniel's ashen face.

"The ranch is on fire."

"The... ranch?" Ainsley surged to her feet as Nat deposited Bella in her arms.

"The house. We're going up. You stay here with the kids. Be safe."

He tore out the door.

Ainsley clung to her little daughter. "We have to help."

"He said stay here." Carey understood why.

"It will take the volunteer fire department the better part of an hour to get up there. By then it could have spread to the stables. To the forest. To the cabins."

Ryder. Was he up at Rockstead? Was he fighting the fire alone right now, waiting for his brothers?

"Viv's up there, too. What can Declan and Ryder and Viv do on their own? Not much."

Bella clung to her mama's neck, crying. How could Ainsley think of leaving her children and running into danger herself?

But Carey wasn't offering to stay with the kids. Not when Ryder might be in danger.

Ainsley grabbed the diaper bag. "Bring Oakley."

"Bring her where? You can't take the girls up there!"

"Dakota's. Riley's. I don't know. Come on!"

THE FIRE HAD a solid foothold when Ryder and Vivienne had returned from a ride up the mountain. He'd called 9-1-1 and then his brothers before leaving Champlain tacked up and ground-tied. The gelding could escape if needed.

Ryder's gut clenched. It wouldn't come to that.

But it could. Crackling flames leaped high into the air from the back of the house.

"What do we do?" Vivienne stood beside him, staring at the fire in shock.

"The guys are coming." But Ryder knew no one could be quick enough to save that house. "There's a fire hose in the pump house. I'll hook it up."

"Then what?"

"We'll pump that creek dry if we need to." He dashed toward the pump house. *It's not going to be enough. It's not going to be enough. It's not going to be enough.*

But he had to do something. Do what he could. How long would it take for his brothers to get here? Where was Dad? His truck was gone.

"Call Dad!" Ryder shouted over his shoulder.

Vivienne dashed into the stable. Good. There was a phone there. Her cell was probably in her cabin, too far away.

Please, God, don't let the fire spread to the cabins. Or to the barn. Or the stables.

The immensity of the disaster coursed through Ryder, but he used it as energy. He yanked the pump house door open and slapped on the light. The folded hose lay on a shelf. The thing weighed a ton, and it was just him.

That was okay. He was strong. Wiry. He could do this. He had to.

He had a new respect for firefighters. He should be doing strength training, not just throwing bales. Throwing calves.

Ryder rolled out the hose then grappled with the connector to the pump. He'd have to disconnect the house line. That meant no water for the animals, either. Well, no decision there. There'd be time for drinking water when they survived this.

How could that coupling supply enough water pressure for the fire hose? How long ago had they tested that hose Dad bought at an auction years ago? What if the mice had gotten to it and chewed holes in it?

Ryder took a deep breath and willed his hands steady as he reefed on the pipe wrench to disconnect the house's plumbing. Finally, he could attach the fire hose. Turn the tap back on. Slowly. He needed to get that hose aimed before it became a living thing in its own right.

"Ryder!"

He shook his head, flinging off the distracting word.

"Ryder! We've got the hose."

He blinked. Looked. Adam stood there, Blake beside him.

"Turn the pressure up!"

He turned, sprinted back into the pump house, and cranked that handle wide open.

"That's a lot of fire!" Travis yelled. "Let's get the horses out of the stable."

"On it!" Noah called back. "Come on, Viv."

Viv. Ryder had forgotten about her. Had she reached Dad? He had to trust that she'd succeeded. There was no time to talk now.

Adam and Blake braced the fire hose and aimed it at the

flames. The fire sizzled and hissed but didn't seem to be otherwise affected.

Where had it started? Kathryn's apartment downstairs? Dad's bedroom above? Upstairs? Did fires only reach upward at first? Then it must have been on the main level.

Something crashed in the house, and a flurry of sparks flew into the night sky. When had it become dark? It had only been dusk when he and Vivienne returned.

Why had they left at all? If they'd been home, they've have seen it sooner. But where was Dad? This monstrosity was *his* house. The boys had all moved out as a statement of independence when they'd established their adulthood.

The sparks flew, but the towering trees had not yet ignited. If the fire crossed the creek, it would burn through that stand of trees like nobody's business.

So far, so good.

Headlights. This time Ryder's sisters-in-law poured out of Ainsley's car.

"What can we do?" Riley yelled.

"Load the truck with tack and get the horses in the trailer," bellowed Adam. "If this fire gets away, the stable will be next."

Then the mammoth stack of hay bales beyond. Most of the feed for all the horses and cattle for the coming winter. Yeah, they'd get another cut of hay, but the best hay came earlier in the growing season.

At least the cows were up in the rangeland. Ryder didn't even want to think what would happen if this started a wildfire blackening thousands of acres despite the forest service's best efforts.

How could a fire have started in Dad's bedroom? Dad didn't smoke. Didn't have a fireplace, not that he'd use it in July if he did. And he wasn't even home.

It didn't make sense.

An electrical fire? But the house wasn't that old. Mom — Monica — had insisted on the enormous house when she married Dad thirty-some years ago. Surely, they'd followed electrical codes. It wasn't like codes had changed that much, right? More load from electronics, but not in Dad's house. Just one computer, and it was in the office on the opposite corner of the house.

Ryder kept moving, checking the creek, checking the valves, checking everything. Didn't know what he was looking for but checking all the same.

If only they had three or four hoses. If only the power would hold, because he wasn't sure the solar batteries held enough juice to pump that much water. Did Dad have another backup system he'd never told the boys about?

Couldn't be. Dad was meticulous about safety. About backups. The solar *was* the backup. Dad wasn't expecting a huge house fire to test all the systems in one go. So, if the fire burned through the electric lines, the lithium-ion batteries had better hold for long enough.

But the fire trucks should be coming soon. Right? How long ago had he called the fire in? It seemed like days. Couldn't be, though.

"Ryder?"

He squinted into the darkness toward Carey's voice.

"Are you okay?"

"No. What are you doing here?" He winced. He sounded rough and ungrateful.

"I was at Ainsley's. I helped empty the tack room. Riley's driving the truck and trailer down to Running Creek."

Ryder looked over at the horse trailer hooked up to Adam's truck. In the glow of the taillights, he watched his brothers load in several of the most skittish horses. The more docile ones were being tied to the back of the trailer.

Carey's hand rested on Ryder's arm. "She'll go real slow, and Vivienne's going to ride in the back and talk to the horses."

He didn't have a better idea. And surely Running Creek was far enough away to be out of danger. He turned back to Carey. "I—"

She brushed her lips over his just as distant sirens wailed.

The fire trucks were coming. Finally.

Riley pulled the truck and trailer off the edge of the driveway to leave room for the incoming equipment. Several of Ryder's brothers mingled with the horses, calming them.

The sirens screamed louder, but what was the point? They'd meet no one on the ranch road, and the horses could do without the provocation. So could the dogs. Sam was howling.

"Ryder? I'm sorry." Carey twined her fingers in his. "When this is over, can we talk?"

He squeezed back. Did he deserve a second chance? Only because she didn't know how badly he'd messed up. But he needed to come clean. "After this. I promise."

The fire engines roared into the yard, and the volunteer force leaped into action, barking commands, following them.

Riley and Vivienne moved the horse parade down the drive, Ainsley's little car behind them. Would they need any more help down at Running Creek to settle the horses?

Maybe he should go. But now that the first rush of adrenaline was through his system, Ryder only wanted to wake up and find he'd had an incredibly vivid nightmare. Except for the part where Carey, once again, stood beside him.

That bit was his wildest hopes come true.

CHAPTER TWENTY

The fire in front of her was the stuff of her worst nightmares. Dakota had kept all the little ones, with Toby and Gavin to help her. Carey had helped Dafne and Ainsley load saddles and bridles and horse blankets into the trucks while the other women worked with the horses. She hadn't ridden in years, and she didn't trust herself calming frightened equines. Not when Riley and Taryn and Vivienne had so much more experience.

Carey clutched her arms around her body. Maybe she should have gone to help with the unloading, but they didn't really need her there. Not that anyone needed her here, either.

Surreal. Firefighters pumped from the creek with minimal shouts, dousing the trees and grass around the perimeter and the stable roof as well as the house itself. They knew what they were doing, but it hadn't stopped Ryder from striding away from her after that brief interlude, looking for a way to help.

There was no 'kid' left in that man's lean body. He moved

with purpose and assurance, doing his best to save his family's home.

Not that there was any hope. Carey could see that, even in her inexperience with fire. The whole structure was engulfed now. Another crash from inside indicated a falling wall. A section of the roof sagged.

Tears stung her eyes, the heat from the blaze drying them as quickly as they tried to form. How would this family rebuild? Declan could go either way. Maybe he'd find a blessing in this disaster, but it was doubtful with his personality. More likely he'd rage like the fire and drive everyone close to him further into retreat.

What would that do to Ryder? Frank's assessment — that Ryder had no education and no ambition beyond cowboying — rang true. If Rockstead ceased operation, Ryder and all his brothers would be left without work.

She couldn't think about that now. The bond they'd re-established moments ago was still fragile, something wrought in the literal heat of disaster. No guarantees it would hold when things cooled off, though Ryder had promised to talk.

That was a start, at least.

A black pickup careened into the yard and skidded to a halt near where Carey stood. The passenger door sprang open, and Kathryn jumped out. She stopped short, her hand clapped over her mouth, her eyes wide.

Carey jogged over and touched her arm. "Aunt Kathryn?"

"Carey? What are you doing here?"

"I was at Ainsley's when the call came."

"Your father..." Kathryn spun and ran toward her boys, joining Declan.

Carey had barely noticed the rancher leaping out of the driver's side. She'd been focused on her aunt. But now Declan grabbed Kathryn in a massive hug, burying his face against her neck. Carey blinked. The man had emotions? He'd let his estranged wife notice them?

They didn't look all that estranged at the moment, that was for sure. Some of the brothers — Carey couldn't make out which ones from the distance — encircled their parents.

A moment later, the fire chief approached the group. Declan, arm still around Kathryn's shoulder, stepped forward and engaged the man.

Why again had Carey stayed when the other women left? She shouldn't have. She had no ride back to Ainsley's. Ryder was busy. And what had Aunt Kathryn meant about Dad?

The flames no longer leaped as high in the air. More of the roof fell. There'd be nothing salvageable. It looked like they'd managed to keep the fire from spreading, though. So that was good… the best possible outcome when it became clear the structure could not be saved.

Carey sank onto the grass. One of the ranch dogs crept up beside her, and she hugged the collie's lean body tight. At least someone needed her.

How long would it take to walk back down to Ainsley's, where she'd left her car? It took a solid fifteen minutes to drive. She wasn't wearing good shoes for that kind of hike and, besides, it was dark. There might be wolves or mountain lions or bears.

She should never have come up here. Shouldn't have stayed.

THE FIREFIGHTERS FOLDED their hoses and stashed their equipment on the ladder trucks.

Ryder stood off to the side, overcome with gratitude for their speed and skill. So long as he didn't look at the smoldering ruins of the house he'd grown up in, he could appreciate how little *other* damage there was to the ranch. His sisters-in-law had moved the horses and tack to safety hours ago, the winter's hay supply was safe, and the cattle grazed far from the home place.

The biggest miracle might be that Dad had cried in Kathryn's arms.

Ryder had definitely not seen that coming, but he couldn't help the surge of hope that came with the sight. A house was easy to rebuild. A broken marriage? Not so much, but Kathryn had consistently laid one brick after another over the past couple of years. Looked like Dad was finally adding bricks of his own.

If Dad and Kathryn could forgive each other and move forward, maybe Ryder and Carey could—

Carey! She'd been here somewhere, right? Had he imagined her hand in his? The touch of her lips? Her apology? Not that she had anything to be sorry for her. It was all on him. Just like the mess of his parents' marriage was all on Dad. Or mostly, anyway.

He pivoted away from his brothers, searching the darkness away from the floodlights from the fire trucks. He'd either dreamed up Carey's presence, or she'd gone with Ainsley and the others. That must be it, because his imagination couldn't have conjured up the whole thing. Not in this adrenaline rush.

A dog whimpered.

Ryder hadn't even stopped to consider the ranch dogs once they'd stopped howling at the sirens. Only Kathryn's Yorkie, Ezra, had ever been a house pet. The others roamed the property, often bedding in the stables near the horses.

They'd have been smart enough to stay away from the fire. But could one have been injured, anyway? Somehow?

He angled toward the sound, his eyes adjusting to the darkness the further he got from the bright beams. There. But it wasn't just the collie he saw, but a woman huddled on the ground beside Sam.

"Carey?" He dropped to the grass beside her. "I thought you'd gone with Ainsley."

She shook her head, her tangled hair half out of her pony-tail, hiding her face.

Ryder tucked his arm around her and drew her closer, only to discover Sam crawling into his lap. "You okay, Sammy? You hurt somewhere?"

The dog whimpered again.

"I-I think he's just scared."

Ryder let out a long breath. "I know how he feels. That was the most terrifying thing I've ever lived through."

"Me, too." Carey's voice trembled.

"Hey, it's okay." He rubbed her upper arm. "No one was hurt. Only the house is gone."

"Only the house?" She sounded incredulous.

He stared into the smoldering pile of debris. "Only that and a bunch of bad memories."

Carey angled her head to look up at him. "What do you mean?"

"The story has it that Monica pushed Dad to build that monstrosity when they were first married. She was all about the prestige."

"But that didn't bring her happiness."

He scoffed a laugh. "Nothing brought her happiness. Not Dad. Not her three sons. Not her marriage to Ed. Not crashing Blake's wedding."

"She won't find it in my father, either. He's no more capable of selflessness than she is."

Was this the time to come clean? Ryder glanced over at the scene in front of the house... or what used to be a house. The fire crew was preparing to leave the scene. He'd be needed with his family momentarily. His secrets had been tightly held for this long; another day wouldn't hurt.

Hurting people hurt people.

Monica was hurting. Jason was hurting. Could they heal each other? It didn't seem likely, but hey, stranger things had happened. More likely they were using each other... but for what?

The rush of the past couple of hours had fled, leaving Ryder's brain like mush. If there was an answer to that question, he wasn't capable of ferreting it out tonight.

Headlights rounded the curve of the driveway, and Ainsley's car pulled to a stop. Vivienne clambered out of the passenger side.

Ryder rose, dumping Sam out of his lap but pulling Carey up with him. "I should talk to Viv. She was amazing. Kept her head."

"I'll get a ride back down with Ainsley. My car's at her place." Carey tugged her hand free and held herself. "I'll see you soon?"

She was pulling back again, but not completely. He wanted to kiss her. Tell her everything. Kiss her again. Propose to her.

Tonight was not the night.

He swept his lips over hers. "Tomorrow. Okay?"

She nodded and hurried over to Ainsley.

Sam bumped his nose into Ryder's hand. Looked like there was a pup who might want a dry shelter to sleep in tonight. Like Ryder's cabin.

Ryder started toward his family but stopped in his tracks. Where would Dad sleep? Everything Declan Cavanagh had ever owned was gone.

No. Not true. The ranch remained. His horse, Diesel, and all the rest of the horses and cows. Dad would rebuild from the ashes.

He could sleep in Ryder's room tonight. Ryder could take the sofa.

"Thanks for the ride back to town." Kathryn sat in Carey's passenger seat. "I wasn't thinking. When the call came, Declan and I just ran for his truck and drove up to the ranch as quickly as we could. I never thought about how I'd get back to town."

"You called the twins, I'm sure."

"Yes, but I feel so awful. I should have been there for them when they found out. Imagine being teens and finding out from your youth pastor that your home is burning, and your mother will be back for you when she can tear herself away from the sight."

"I don't think that's how it was." Carey had seen Declan cradling Kathryn close. Had seen them crying together.

"Probably close enough, from their perspective." Kathryn sighed. "I can't believe how tired I am, now that it's all over but the mop-up. I'll take the girls up tomorrow and we can help with that."

"I was glad to see you and Declan together," Carey offered.

"Our relationship has been coming along. I thought I'd blown it earlier tonight, though. Was that only a few hours ago?"

Carey didn't need to answer as she turned onto the gravel road at the base of the ranch lane.

"I invited your father and Monica over for tea tonight. I didn't tell Declan. I'm not sure what I was thinking. That we could clear the air and all be some sort of friends?"

Carey turned her snort into a cough.

"Exactly. They never made it up to the apartment. Declan nearly punched your father in the face in the parking lot."

Not an unbelievable scenario, by any means.

Kathryn turned to Carey in her seat. "They kept talking about tying up loose ends. I can't, for the life of me, figure out what they meant."

"They said that to me, too, when we had dinner together a few nights ago."

"To make up with you and Laurel, maybe?"

Carey shook her head. "If so, I couldn't see any evidence. Dad was just as full of himself as ever. I hadn't ever conversed with Monica before, but she didn't seem all that conciliatory, either."

"So, you're not the loose end they were talking about. And Monica hasn't contacted any of the boys."

Carey had wondered about that. She narrowed her gaze at the 'Welcome to Jewel Lake' sign as they passed it. "So, what *were* they talking about?"

Kathryn gasped and slapped her hand over her mouth. "No way."

Carey angled a look at her aunt, but there were no tangible clues.

"Could they have been responsible for the fire?"

"What?" Carey's brain went into overdrive, processing the progression of the disaster that she'd seen. "It started at the back, I think, on the driveway side. I'm not familiar with the layout, but I assume that's where the kitchen is? Or maybe... maybe a fire from lint build-up in the dryer? I hear that can happen if people don't clean the filters regularly."

Kathryn shook her head. "Those rooms aren't at the back of the house. The kitchen is in the middle of the main floor. The master bedroom is at the back, though, overlooking the creek."

"A fireplace?" Carey tried again.

"There isn't one in that end of the house." Kathryn gulped. "And the suite the boys built me is below the master bedroom. It opens onto my garden..." Her voice caught. "My refuge."

Carey gripped the steering wheel tightly as she turned off the highway. "My dad wouldn't know about that. Monica wouldn't, either." Would she?

"Should I call the police? But I have no proof."

"Did the fire chief give any indication of how it might have started?"

Kathryn shook her head. "They'll go through the... the ashes... when they've cooled off some. I can't believe the house is gone." She rubbed her eyes as a sob broke out.

How could Carey leave Kathryn to debrief her daughters by herself? She couldn't. Kathryn was her aunt. Alexia and Emma her cousins. Even if nothing came of things with Ryder, she was still bonded to the Cavanaghs.

For better. For worse.

CHAPTER TWENTY-ONE

T ake my bed, Dad."

"No. I couldn't put you out."

"I've got a sleeping bag. My sofa's long enough."

"But—" Dad still had a sort of haunted look in his eyes.

Ryder nudged his dad's arm with his elbow. "I'm not taking no for an answer. It's nearly midnight. There's nothing we can do here until things cool off." Not that there'd be much salvageable. If anything. "Tomorrow's soon enough to start making decisions."

Dad looked every one of his fifty-eight years as Ryder led him away. Looked like another thirty had been added on, honestly.

Vivienne stepped closer out of the shadows. "I can't believe that happened."

Dad glanced at her. "Any idea how it did?"

He'd better not be blaming her.

"Ry and I had gone for a ride to check up on the yearlings in the lower pasture. Came back, and the whole back corner was ablaze."

"You rescued the horses."

Vivienne's chin came up just a little. "Riley and Taryn knew what to do. We all helped get them down to Running Creek."

"I'm glad—" Dad seemed about to choke on his words. "I'm glad you were here."

"Thanks." Vivienne blinked a few times.

Ryder nearly did the same. Stranger words Declan Cavanagh had never uttered.

"You want to be a nurse, huh?"

"Yes, sir. Or maybe a nurse practitioner."

"What school?"

"I'm accepted at MSU, Bozeman campus."

"I'll write you a check tomorrow." Dad's shoulders sagged.

"Thanks, Decl… Dad." Vivienne turned away, sounding a little shook up.

Would Dad's finances be tied up with the insurance claim? Guess he'd figure it out. Tomorrow was soon enough for that, too.

Ryder slung his arm around his kid sister's shoulder and squeezed. "You did good, Viv. Sleep well, and see you in the morning."

"Yeah. Thanks. Has anyone let Cook know?"

Ryder inhaled sharply. There'd been an emergency with Cook's daughter in Nevada, and she'd taken off for a few days. "Not that I know of. I sure didn't think of it. She's due back, when, Monday?"

"I think so."

"I'll call her tomorrow." Tomorrow would be a mighty full day. "Come on, Dad."

"I don't want to put you out."

That was a first. Ryder eyed his father. "Don't make me try

to take you. I'm not sure I can." Dad might have thirty-some years on him, but the man was built like a bull.

Dad huffed a laugh. "Okay. Just for tonight. We'll figure it out…"

"Tomorrow. I know."

Vivienne turned off at her cabin, and Ryder walked his dad to the one two doors up.

"Sammy?" There was a hitch to Dad's voice at the sight of the collie on Ryder's doorstep. "You okay, boy?"

"The dogs are smart. I saw Dingo, too, but she was skittish."

Ryder flipped on his light, thankful once again that the fire hadn't engulfed the main powerlines. "Want a cup of tea? I've got a few kinds. And Cook sent a carton of cookies over before she left."

"Sounds good." Dad dropped into one of the two wooden chairs beside the table and cradled his head in his hands. "You don't have to look after me like this."

"Sure, I do. We're family. It's what family does." Ryder filled his kettle with water. Good thing Travis had remembered to switch the hoses again after the fire trucks left.

"I didn't treat you kids right."

Did they really need to get into this in the aftermath of a life-changing event? Maybe they did.

"I never figured out why you boys would rather live in one of these dumpy cabins than in that big house once you got older."

Independence. Or at least as much as they were going to get, still working for the brand.

"Now I guess I'll find out the allure. One of these is going to be my home for a while, huh?"

"Looks like. There's three empty, so you can take your

pick. Blake's probably has the most furniture and stuff left in it. We can check tomorrow."

"Yeah. Tomorrow."

"Black tea? Or maybe something herbal with no caffeine?"

"Nothing will keep me awake."

Ryder wasn't so sure. Those searing flames were going to leap in his mind's eye all night long. He pulled out a couple of chamomile teabags. "Let's not chance it." He loaded a plate with a dozen cookies and set it on the table.

So weird. Who'd ever have thought he'd have his father over for tea, cookies, and a slumber party? It had taken a crisis. For once, it looked like Declan Cavanagh was reacting appropriately in a crisis situation. Humbly. Thankfully. Generously, at least with Viv.

"I can't figure what started that thing."

"The fire chief will send someone out in the next day or two to look for clues."

"Yeah. He said."

Ryder poured boiling water over the teabags he'd dropped in the mugs. "I was surprised to see Kathryn riding with you."

Dad rubbed his soot-covered face. "We'd been at her place. That darn woman." He shook his head but didn't sound angry. "You know what she did?"

"Tell me." Ryder braced himself.

"You're just like her, you know. Figure tea and cookies will make everything better." Dad plucked a morsel off the plate and took a big bite.

"She taught me well, I guess." Ryder couldn't help a grin.

"She invited your mother and Jason over. I guess she figured we could all have a nice chitchat and end as friends? I have no idea what she was thinking."

"Sounds like Kathryn."

"I nearly popped that pompous jerk in the nose." Dad inhaled the rest of the cookie and reached for another.

Ryder held his breath. Waited for more.

"Anyway, they left. Then Kathryn and I had a talk. Overdue, I guess."

Didn't it figure that a call about the house fire would break up a moment like that? But by the looks of them together in front of the blaze, the disaster might have driven them closer together, not farther apart.

"Then you called." Dad shoved the rest of the cookie into his mouth.

Ryder sat across from him. "You asked why we boys moved out of the house as quickly as we could."

Dad eyed him. "Yeah?"

"So many negative memories there. Of you and Mom yelling and throwing things."

"You remember that?" Dad winced.

"A little. Travis and Blake definitely do. And then... well, everything. A bit of peace when Kathryn came and when the twins were little. And then the negativity started again."

"I screwed up a thousand times."

Hard to deny. "We all do, I guess. That's why Jesus came. To save us from ourselves."

"Now you're sounding like her again."

"She taught me well, I guess." If the words were good once, they were good twice. "She's pretty amazing."

"I see that now." Dad huffed. "I don't know. I was angry all the time. I figured if I could drive your mother away like that, I could do the same with Kathryn."

Ryder's eyebrows shot up. "You wanted her to leave?"

"No? Yes? I don't know. I just had to push all the buttons and find out where the edges were."

"Like Toby or Gavin."

"Didn't say it was the smartest thing I ever did." Dad shook his head. "That might have been marrying Kathryn."

Hard to argue. "Might've been."

"So, yeah. That house. You're right. It doesn't hold many good memories. Maybe it's okay it's gone. Can get a fresh start and all that. If only Kathryn…"

"She loves you, you know."

Dad pulled in a long breath and let it out slowly. Then he eyed Ryder. "I don't imagine your pajamas are much bigger than you are. I could use a shower and some shut-eye."

The thought of Dad squishing into Ryder's clothes was laughable. "Let me run through the other cabins and see if Travis or Blake left anything behind. They're closer to your size."

"Yeah. Thanks."

Had Declan Cavanagh ever thanked one of his sons for anything at all before this? Not that Ryder could recall.

"Be back in a minute." He grabbed his flashlight and headed out, Sam at his side.

"Did you hear about the huge fire at Rockstead last night?"

Carey groaned into her pillow. Why had she answered her phone without checking the caller ID, again? Because she wasn't up for Stephanie. "Yeah. I was there. I saw it."

"Oh, girl! I need the deets."

"It's only…" Carey checked her watch. "…nine in the morning."

"You say that as though it's early. I've been up three hours."

"It's early when I was up there until nearly midnight."

"What happened? How did it start? How much damage was there?"

"The house is gone. Everything else seemed okay." Carey laid back against her pillow, frowning. "Why are you really calling? Because something must be going on if you've been up since six on a Saturday."

Stephanie burst into tears.

Oh, boy. Carey waited. Some days she wondered if it was worth being friends with someone who so passionately loved someone who didn't love her back. There was a lot of drama.

"He's dating Harper."

And the entire congregation of Creekside Fellowship — indeed, the entire population of Jewel Lake — could have seen that coming. "I thought you were over Eli."

Stephanie sobbed.

Okay, fine, Carey was awake now. She needed to pee. And she needed a hot cuppa in the worst way. "Steph?"

"I thought he'd remember why he asked me out in the first place. It was Valentine's Day…"

Rumor had it Eli had asked Stephanie out to distract himself from unsuitable Harper. He'd hoped to fall in love with Stephanie, but instead Harper had become a believer and he'd let himself fall for his true love. It all sounded so romantic if you were talking to someone other than Stephanie.

But Carey was talking to Stephanie. "It wasn't meant to be. God has someone else for you. Be patient. Keep being as awesome as you already are."

"Not helping. Someone else isn't Eli."

"Stephanie? You have to let him go. Totally."

Her friend sniffled. "Harper's so nice. It's hard to be angry with her. It's not like she tried to break us up."

This was sounding a little more promising.

"So, I forgive her."

"Good."

"Forgiving Eli might take a little longer."

"You need to—"

"I know. Let it go. But…"

"Stephanie."

Her friend sighed. "I'm trying, okay? I really am. Every time I think I'm making progress, he stabs me anew."

Drama, much?

"You know what I mean. Ryder's playing with your affections the same way Eli did with mine."

"Um, no. Not the same at all." Though she still didn't know what had happened to cause Ryder to pull back. "We're talking. We'll work things out. The fire took up kind of a lot of his attention last night."

"Keep telling yourself that."

"Stephanie, just because things didn't work out for you and Eli, doesn't mean everyone else is doomed to break up, too."

"Your father and Ryder's mother. That must be awkward."

Carey stiffened. "Not the nicest surprise, no. But what they do has no impact on us."

"Please. They've been seen together all over town. They've been eating at the Golden Grill nearly every meal and talking it up with Estelle. You know that's almost like taking out a full-page ad in the Gazette."

Hmm. Did Kathryn's suspicions have any foundation? Maybe Carey should find out what Estelle knew.

Or she could wait and see what the investigators found. It wasn't really any of her business. And if her father happened to be responsible? Maybe she didn't really want to know any sooner than she had to.

Someone buzzed to be let into the building. Carey's heart jumped. Ryder? Unlikely. He'd probably been up much later than she had. "I've got to go, Stephanie. Talk to you later."

She pressed the intercom button. "Hello?"

"Sis, we need to talk."

Laurel. What bee was in her sister's bonnet this time?

"Good morning to you, too. Ever heard of phoning?"

"Pfft. Like you'd answer. Let me in already."

Carey rolled her eyes, released the security lock, and opened her own door so nothing would impede Laurel's progress.

"Dad and Monica are gone!"

That was the big, exciting news? "If they ever planned to stay, I hadn't heard about it."

Laurel waved her hand impatiently. "We were going to do breakfast before they headed east. I was waiting at Denny's, and they didn't come, so I called Dad. And he said oops, sorry, they'd decided to leave early and were already in North Dakota!"

"That's not leaving early. That's driving through the night."

"I know, right? Why didn't he tell me? It was going so well."

Carey's eyebrows arched. "So well? He was being a jerk, and so was she."

"Just because you're dating her son. The family refuses to see her side of the breakup. Can you imagine being married to Declan Cavanagh? No wonder she left."

So not going there. Carey shuddered. "Sounds like you've seen more of Dad this trip than I have."

Laurel's gaze shifted to the window then back. "Sorry? You seemed busy."

"Whatever." Carey had spent enough time to know she didn't want more. "That's all he had to say for himself? *Oops, sorry?*"

"He sounded so casual."

"I need to talk to Aunt Kathryn. You coming with me or going back to Missoula?"

"Aunt *Kathryn*? What does she have to do with anything?"

"Maybe nothing, but let's find out."

CHAPTER TWENTY-TWO

I t was afternoon before Ryder could get away. Dafne had brought breakfast up to the ranch. Taryn had followed with lunch. They couldn't go on this way indefinitely, but at least it was an option for now. Cook was going to need more than a cabin kitchenette to feed them all when she returned.

Dad was heading down to town, too. The man needed to start the insurance process, but meanwhile, he needed clothes as well as bedding and other supplies for cabin three. Blake had left it partially furnished, so that was a help.

Ryder had moved everything he cared about from his old room in the house a couple of years ago. No, his trip into Jewel Lake was for Carey. And he was driving slowly.

"God?" Sometimes it helped if he prayed aloud. "I don't deserve another chance with Carey. I have no sense how this is going to go. If she'll forgive me or kick me out on my butt." Just the thought made him go cold. "If You could just prepare the way. Give me the words to apologize properly. To make it up to her in some way."

He slowed even more as he drove past his brothers' houses. Gavin and Toby were shooting baskets on the side of Blake and Dafne's garage. Gavin was basketball crazy. Apparently, it was a big thing in Spokane where he'd lived before his mom took a teaching job in Jewel Lake and fell in love with Blake. Looked like Gavin might be getting Toby hooked, too.

His cell rang when he turned onto the highway, and he tapped his Bluetooth button to receive the call.

"Just hear me out."

"Branson. Stop."

"No. You know how my mom and Estelle Mulligan are friends? Mom says Estelle says Jason let on he's going to get even with your dad."

Ryder let out a breath. "Old news."

"I mean it... what?"

"The ranch house up at Rockstead burned to the ground last night. Nobody was inside." Thank the Lord for that.

"No way. I didn't want to be right."

"Yeah. I wish you weren't, either. What's stuck in that guy's craw, anyway?"

"Besides your mother?"

"It's been longer than that, unless they've been secretly together for like a dozen years. Which could be, maybe. How would I know?"

"Anyway, I'm guessing Estelle might be willing to stand witness if it's helpful. And Ry? I'm sorry."

Ryder sighed. "Me, too. It hasn't been my home for a few years, but it was still hard to see it engulfed in flames. It's just a pile of smoking ash this morning. Rocks from the fireplace, a few charred beams, and I think I saw a twisted appliance or two in the wreckage."

"Oh, man. That's a heck of a way to get even."

"My mother probably helped think it up. Until they connected, Jason hadn't been back in Montana for years."

"Connected? Or *reconnected*?"

Gears clicked. "Could be that, too. I don't know. I didn't get much sleep last night. I gave my bed to Dad and slept on the sofa. Such as it was."

"Call me when things shake down? If that goes to trial, I'd like to be around to see it."

Munching popcorn in the gallery as though it were just another show? No. Branson was better than that. Fixated, sure, but better.

"Yeah. I'll let you know. And Bran?"

"Hmm?"

"I'm almost to Carey's apartment. Could you, you know, say a prayer for me? Because I really, really like this girl, and I'm about to tell her everything."

"Everything? You must be serious."

"Very."

"I'm sorry if I messed it up for you."

"It wasn't you, at least, not mostly. I started it. You just followed through." And through. And through. But he wasn't going to throw that back in Branson's face now. Doggedness was likely an excellent quality in an attorney.

They closed the call, and Ryder drove the rest of the way to the apartment building in silence. He pulled in, parked, and looked up at Kathryn's windows. Did he need to check in with her first? How were Emma and Alexia taking the news?

In answer to his question, the living room draperies shifted. Before he'd locked his truck and crossed the parking lot, the building door burst open and the twins exploded out, launching at him.

"Whoa, you two!" He grabbed one girl with each arm and tugged them in.

"Our house burned *down*?" Alexia asked in disbelief.

"All the way."

"I still had stuff there I wanted."

"Me, too." Emma hiccupped into Ryder's shoulder.

"I'm sorry, but there's nothing salvageable." Maybe he should soften the blow, but Kathryn had obviously already told them everything. He was only a corroborator.

"I was hoping Mom and Dad would get back together." Emma sniffled. "Now we don't even have a house."

"They can build a new one." Ryder rubbed Emma's shoulder.

"It's better if we live in town until we're out of school, anyway," Alexia said. "We missed a lot of stuff living at the ranch."

"I miss being at home. Can you take me to see, Ry?"

"I'll talk to your mom about it, okay?"

"Mom and Dad are going shopping," Alexia put in. "I can't imagine Dad living in one of those little cabins."

Ryder couldn't, either. But then, he could scarcely believe the house was gone. His imagination was stuck on that reality.

"Maybe he'll live with us here."

Lex rolled her eyes. "Don't be such a baby, Em. That's not how it works when couples are *taking a break*." She finger-quoted it.

Ryder nudged Alexia with his elbow. "It's not being a baby to wish your parents loved each other and lived together."

She gave him a mock shocked look. "You want your mother back?"

"Monica? Not a chance. But your mom is pretty much mine, you know. She's been my mom since I was younger than Toby and Gavin. And I miss her and Dad being together, too."

"I'm so glad you came to see us, Ry." Emma clung to his arm. "I needed a big brother today."

"I... uh..."

"He's here to see Carey, dummy."

"You are?"

Ryder hugged Emma tight. "I am. But I'll stop by before I leave, okay?"

"Okay."

Was he doing the right thing, leaving his kid sisters to weather this without him and go to Carey instead? Yeah. They had their mom, and Dad would be by soon, if he'd asked Kathryn to help him set up a cabin. Maybe the girls would go along.

He chuckled as he mounted the steps and Alexia keyed the three of them in. Speaking of imagination, he could just see how bored Lex would be in ten minutes flat choosing new jeans and shirts for Dad.

But that wasn't his problem. His problem was the mess he'd made of his relationship with Carey.

Time to man up.

This time, it was a brisk knock on her door. Did no one use the entry buzzer anymore?

Carey huffed but peeked through the peephole.

Ryder.

She ran her clammy hands down her flared skirt. Too much? Too late if it was. She whipped the door open. "Hi."

"Carey." He grasped both her hands, and his gaze took her in. "You look great."

"Thanks." Maybe her outfit wasn't over the top, after all. "I'd say the same to you... okay, I will. You look great."

He grinned. "But I look tired. I get it." He came into the apartment and shut the door. "Dad stayed with me last night. He... he wanted to talk."

"You say that like it's unusual."

"Very. Conversation with Dad my entire life has been like, 'go do this or that, boy,' and me saying, 'yes, sir,' in response."

"I'm glad if that's something good that comes from the fire."

"Me, too. I think there's hope."

"Kathryn thinks so, too."

His eyebrows angled up.

"Remember I gave her a ride back last night. We had time to talk."

"I keep forgetting she's your aunt." He grimaced. "Once, that was a much bigger deal in my mind."

"Mine, too." She stepped closer. Reached for his hand, but somehow it wasn't within easy reach. How had they held hands last night? How had he kissed even the top of her head?

"May I sit down?"

"So formal," she teased. But yeah, he wasn't amused. She gestured toward the living area. Whatever he needed to talk about, he was taking it seriously. She should be, too. It had come between them before, but at least, this time he was willing to explain.

She breathed a prayer as she perched in the Victorian tub chair while he settled his angular body on the sofa.

Ryder leaned forward with his elbows on his knees and his hands clasped together. "I don't know how to say this."

"You're scaring me."

He took a deep breath. "You know, a few things came to light a couple of years ago when Ainsley and Vivienne found us. When we realized Vivienne was Declan's daughter."

Carey nodded. She'd spent a bit of time worried that Vivienne might be her own half-sister. After all, Brenda Johnson had worked for Dad in that time period. The time when Mom and Dad's marriage folded, Uncle Joe died... so much had gone down within the space of a year or two.

"There were things — there's no easy way to say this." Ryder surged to his feet, crossed to the window, then pivoted again, hands clenched behind his back. "Your dad... you know he tried to take advantage of Kathryn, right? He wanted a piece of Joe's legacy. No. That's not quite right."

Carey dared to take a breath.

"He wanted all of it, or so it seemed. He tried to get Joe to sign paperwork when he was dying. Paperwork that would have willed Running Creek to him and left Kathryn and their sons out in the cold."

"Nooo. But he didn't succeed, right?" Still, stars spun in Carey's peripheral vision.

"Joe wasn't too far gone at that point. He read the fine print. Tore up the papers."

"Whew. I'm sorry, Ryder. I know it wasn't my fault; I was only a little kid, but—"

"There's more."

"Oh." She folded her hands in her lap and sat up straighter. Braced herself. "Tell me."

"When Joe died, Jason was up at the ranch all the time, pestering Kathryn to marry him. Said he'd take care of everything."

Carey winced. How embarrassing, but not shocking. Not after the way he'd acted this week with Monica.

"Declan found out and basically rescued Kathryn. She deeded Running Creek to him. He adopted Adam, Noah, and Nathaniel. Your dad backed off."

By the flatness in Ryder's voice, he still wasn't done. Was she allowed to be happy that Dad had enough sense to realize when he was beat and not pursue his sister-in-law when she was married to someone else?

"Not long after, Jason left town, and rumors filtered back that he'd come into some money. It made us suspicious that he'd found a way to fleece Kathryn after all. Or... someone else." Ryder scrunched his eyes for a few seconds then refocused on her. "At least, it made *me* suspicious."

Carey stared at him. Meaning... what, exactly?

"I got talking with my buddy Branson deWitt. I don't know if you remember the deWitt family. Bran and I knew each other in youth group at Creekside, but that was long after you'd moved away with your mom."

Branson deWitt? Why did that sound familiar? Oh! "That's the guy who's been poking around, asking Laurel questions about Dad."

Ryder let out a long shuddering breath. "He's in law school. He's fascinated by all kinds of fraud. Insurance fraud. Other types. When I mentioned that things seemed weird, he jumped on it. Offered to do some poking around. I... I let him. No. I encouraged him."

"You had my father investigated." Carey slowly rose to her feet.

"I did. And I'm sorry. I didn't realize Branson wouldn't let it go. I've tried to call him off several times, but he was like Sammy with a bone."

"You could have just asked me where Dad got his money from."

"I know the story now. How his great-aunt died and left him the cottage but not a lot of cash. And..." Ryder blinked hard. "Branson verified the existence of the great-aunt. That it wasn't just a story he made up."

Carey hadn't even thought of the fact Dad might have lied. But of course, why wouldn't he? He'd lied about so much else. "My dad's a jerk, and my aunt thinks he might have been the one to set the fire."

"That's what Branson thinks, too."

Her eyebrows shot up of their own accord. "The fire was last night. I thought you said you called him off."

"I told you I tried. The night you first invited me for dinner. And the night of the festival."

"After you found out Dad was coming to visit. You thought something might give your investigation away."

"Carey, when all this started, I didn't think I stood a chance with you. I was too young for you, we're sort of shirt-tail relations, and I didn't think you'd ever look twice at me."

"We've been over all that."

"We have. This was before. By then... I was caught up in this thing with Bran. I knew that would kill any chance I might have had with you. It was idle curiosity at first, but it wasn't any of my business. My brothers told me to leave it. Kathryn told me to leave it. But I didn't, until I realized what it had snowballed into. And that my feelings for you had also grown, and Carey, I love you, and I've hurt you, and if you needed any proof I'm too young and immature for a woman like you, now you have it."

She took a few steps toward him, but he was staring at the floor and didn't notice. Then she closed the distance and pulled his hands from behind his back, gripping them tightly between her own. "Ryder."

"I'm sorry. I can't tell you how sorry."

"Ryder. Were you wrong in your suspicions?"

"Yes. And, also, no. But I shouldn't have—"

"Ryder, I love you."

His head tipped up so slowly Carey could hardly stand it. Finally, his tortured eyes met hers. "Don't mess with me," he said hoarsely.

"I'm not."

"But..."

"Ryder, it takes a man to admit when he's wrong. I can see how a person could get sucked down a trail like that. Part of me wants to stick up for my dad, to put on my rose-tinted glasses and pretend he could never have been like that, but I know better. I agree that it seems like he — and your mother — might have attempted to tie up a loose end last night by getting Declan where it hurts."

Ryder shook his head. "They missed the mark."

"Oh?"

"They should have gone for the stable, in that case, not the house. Or, even worse, gone for Kathryn. Because as unbelievable as it may seem, Declan loves her."

"I'm glad. Because I know she loves him." She gripped his hands more tightly.

His eyes searched hers. "You know who else loves someone?"

Her breath fled. "Who?"

"Me. I love you."

Since she'd already expressed her feelings on the matter, she simply tilted her face toward his.

He cupped her face between his palms, thumbs tracing her cheekbones. Then he lowered his mouth to hers and kissed her gently. Too gently.

Carey grasped the collars of his shirt and showed him how she wanted to be kissed.

CHAPTER TWENTY-THREE

I can't believe I haven't taken you up here before." Ryder swept his hand to point out the entire vista. From this vantage point, the peaks of Glacier National Park to the north peeked between the lower mountains. The trees in the high places were starting to turn gold.

It was September now, and they'd been dating openly for over a month. They'd managed a few shorter rides from Running Creek, since Dad had decided that, while the stable was empty, they might as well give it a thorough floor-to-ceiling scrubbing. They'd also repainted most of the interior in a washable, high-gloss white to make future cleaning easier. Now the fumes had dissipated, and they'd finally moved the horses back to the Rockstead stable.

And that meant easier access to Ryder's favorite vistas. He'd packed a picnic and planned to show Carey the trappers cabin. He and Blake would be coming up weekends for hunting this fall. There was nothing like a freezer full of venison and elk.

Carey, mounted on Kathryn's mare, Laire, looked around her, eyes wide. "It's... beautiful."

"Not as beautiful as you."

She rolled her eyes. "I'm serious."

"So am I." Ryder nudged Champlain closer with his knee and stretched to kiss her lightly. The distance between riders was the greatest downfall of riding horseback with one's girlfriend. It might also be a blessing. It wasn't like they didn't spend a lot of time kissing.

"I don't see you in jeans very often."

Carey laughed. "You might make a cowgirl out of me yet." She lifted her hot pink cowboy hat. "I can't believe you bought this for me. It was *your* birthday, not mine."

"It's not every day a guy turns twenty-five. He should be able to celebrate by getting his favorite girl something special." He kissed her again then recentered himself on Champlain's back. "We're about half an hour from the cabin. You good for it, or do you want to stop and stretch a bit?" He waggled his eyebrows suggestively.

"Stretch, huh?" Her laughing eyes met his. "Maybe we'd better keep going."

"Fair enough." Ryder turned to scan the trail in front of them.

A doe flashed the underside of her tail at them as she bounded into the trees.

"Oooh. I don't often see them in the wild," Carey breathed.

"No, just wandering around town eating people's lilies three feet from their back doors."

She laughed. "That's true. They're so much more magnificent in their natural habitat."

"Aren't they, though?"

Carey glanced over as the horses plodded up the trail. "I still can't believe my dad is in jail."

Ryder winced. "Or my mother. Or that she remembered that back trail up to the ranch. No one's used it for years, not since Travis used to sneak to town as a teenager."

"Arson is really serious. Ten years." She bit her lip. "He gave the keys to his cottage to Laurel."

This was news. "Is she moving out there? What's she going to do in Maine?"

"I don't know that she's moving permanently, but she's planning on going for a few months. This is the last time of year I'd want to go. Imagine the New England coast in winter. Cold, foggy, clammy. Ugh."

Note: don't marry Carey in winter and take her to New England for a honeymoon.

Ryder swallowed hard. Yeah, his mind was going there, but it seemed too early to propose. What was he afraid of, that she'd say no? Maybe it was that old *age* thing still rearing up in his mind. It shouldn't, but sometimes it snuck out and messed with his brain. At least he'd finally come clean about the investigation.

"You know how you didn't tell me about looking into my father?"

What, now she was a mind-reader? "Yeah?" he replied cautiously.

"I'm glad I didn't know at first. I would have defended him. It would have been dumb, but it's still true. Even though we didn't have a warm, fuzzy father-daughter relationship, I wanted to see the best in him."

"That's a good quality. But I'm sorry — again — that it happened at all."

"Without Branson's records, the whole investigation

would have taken longer. Dad and your mom might have had time to disappear. As it was, they were pretty surprised to be arrested before they even made it back to Maine."

"But they didn't find any evidence he'd manipulated his insurance company, and that's what I originally suspected."

"You know what I love about you?"

She was going there, right this minute, when he was already uncomfortable at the topic at hand? How long would it take before he wouldn't feel burning shame that he'd allowed his youthful curiosity to override his good sense? Finally, he got the word out. "What?"

"I love your sense of fairness. Of justice. You see something wrong, and you want to make it right."

Hmm. Put *that* way...

"When Alexia and Emma are at each other's throats, you see both sides and get them to call a truce."

"I thought they'd be better friends at seventeen than they are."

Carey shook her head. "They had no one but each other for the first fifteen years. Once their worlds opened up, it's not surprising they'd experience it differently. Their personalities are so unique."

"I guess." He angled a look at her. "Want to know something I love about you?"

She chuckled. "What?"

"That you're an even-keeled thinker. And I love that you love my sisters, and not just because they're your cousins."

"It's always going to be complicated, isn't it?"

"Always. The Cavanagh clan is nothing if not convoluted. When I was younger, I didn't think there'd ever be a time it felt like a family. Dad and Kathryn weren't getting along, Travis and Adam were at each other's throats until Adam left in a huff to try his luck on the rodeo circuit. Blake was obnoxious and rude all the time, and Noah and Nathaniel were in their own little world that no one else was allowed into." Ryder took a deep breath. "The girls were too little to be the kind of company I needed. I felt isolated. Alone. All that in the midst of a family of eight kids."

"At my house, it was just me and Laurel. We stuck together — she's only a couple of years older than I am — and I found a lot of solace in reading."

"Reading?" Ryder offered her a mock shocked look. "That's not real life."

"My point exactly. It was nice to get away from reality to a world where heroines were feisty and not drab, awkward girls—"

"Drab? Awkward?" Ryder interrupted. "Never you. Not a chance."

"Oh, but I was." She glanced at him. "I still feel that way."

And Ryder vowed he'd change her perception of herself. She'd see what he saw. How authentic and beautiful and sweet she really was.

THE SUN ANGLED low through the trees and cast a golden glow on the ranch yard as Carey's and Ryder's horses walked toward the stable hours later.

It had been a beautiful day, full of enough kisses and sweet endearments to satisfy Carey's needy soul for a bit longer. Ryder loved her. Every time she thought those words, her heart felt like it expanded a teensy bit more. If she thought it a thousand times, her heart would explode, and that would be quite a mess.

But Ryder excelled in cleaning up messes, just as he'd mopped up the lemonade from Ainsley and Nat's floor all those months ago. He didn't stop to ask whose job it was, or figure such things were beneath him. He just stepped in.

She loved him. One day, he'd ask her to marry him, right? And she'd say yes.

Would it be as romantic a moment as in a Georgette Heyer Regency romance? Although Freddy Standen in *Cotillion* hadn't proposed all that romantically. Kitty Charing had lured him into a fake engagement to make his cousin jealous, but it had backfired on all of them. The other guy had been too much of a womanizing jerk for Kitty all along, and she'd realized she was actually in love with Freddy, whose sideways comment that they should make the fake into real had actually been a proposal.

What about that had seemed romantic to her when she was a tween? Or the other dozen times she'd read her favorite story?

Carey angled a glance at Ryder, who sat tall on the dappled horse beside her. He was all testosterone in a way a pampered Regency lord could never be. No cravat that took an hour to style, no silk breeches or gleaming Hessian boots. Just an honest-to-goodness cowboy in scuffed western boots, worn blue jeans, a denim shirt, and a Stetson.

Her heart swelled. She'd much rather live in Montana in the twenty-first century than in Regency England. How tedious it must have been, ball after opera after soiree.

Ryder dismounted at the corral and immediately reached for her. How romantic was that? She turned into his arms and kissed him. Champlain whinnied in her ear, and she laughed.

"Guess we should put the horses away," Ryder said with a grin. "Want to curry?"

"Sure." That meant he'd remove the heavy saddles. She'd let him, though one of these days she'd learn how. Because, Lord willing, there would be many more horseback rides together in their future.

When they emerged from the stable a while later, Carey saw her aunt's car parked near the remains of the ranch house. Kathryn and Declan stood nearby, arms around each other.

Speaking of romance...

Kathryn turned at the sound of the stable door closing and beckoned them over.

Ryder clasped Carey's hand in his as they strolled toward his parents.

"Have a good ride?" Kathryn asked.

"We did. What an amazing view from up by the cabin!"

"I love it, too." Kathryn turned to Declan. "Shall we let the kids know?"

He nodded and studied the two of them long enough for Carey to get nervous. But Declan wasn't going to yell at her or hit her or anything like that. He might once have had a temper, but since the housefire — and maybe a while before that — he seemed to be a much more restrained man.

"That was a mighty big house." Declan waved toward the ruins. "I don't know why I let Monica talk me into it."

Carey couldn't answer. The woman must have been persuasive, because it seemed she'd been the force that convinced Dad arson was a great way of getting even.

"Anyway, it's gone, and the insurance check is finally on its way. I don't want the same thing again."

"Makes sense, Dad." Ryder's fingers tightened around Carey's. "What do you have in mind?"

His parents glanced at each other and seemed to have a

silent conversation. Wasn't that the mark of a couple on the same footing? Carey tucked the thought away.

"Well, first off, we talked to Cook. I've sure appreciated her all these years, but we don't have a gang that needs feeding all the time anymore." Declan looked at Kathryn, and she took up the thread.

"Her daughter's situation has changed, too. Long story short, Cathleen would like to stay in Nevada and help care for her grandchildren."

"Oh, boy. Who's going to cook?"

Carey elbowed him. "You could learn. All of you could. Vivienne already knows how, but don't stick it all on her."

Kathryn smiled. "As your dad was saying, we're not going to build a huge house again. We're thinking a three-bedroom bungalow, all one level, since we're not getting any younger, and—"

"We?" Ryder interrupted. "Are you two…?"

Kathryn rested her head on Declan's shoulder. "It's a process, but we're working through it."

"I've got a lot to learn." Declan shook his head. "This place — the ranch, the house, the regard of the community — was everything to me. I didn't care who I stepped on as I climbed up, because I wasn't coming back down."

Carey studied Ryder's dad. This looked real. He seemed sad yet also at peace. Authentically so.

"So, the house is gone. The prestige is fleeting. It doesn't matter, not at all. I missed what was important for far too long." He cut his gaze toward his wife. "Not just Kathryn, though why she stood by me for all those years, I'll never know."

"The amazing grace of God," Kathryn murmured. "He hadn't given up on you, so how could I?"

"And that's the crux, right there. God…" Declan shook his head.

"Dad?"

Carey could hear the hope in Ryder's voice.

"Yeah. God got me. I've been such a fool; I can't even tell you." The man grunted. "I guess I don't need to. You've seen it all your life. I'm sorry, son."

Ryder let go of Carey and closed the gap with his father, who released Kathryn as they met in the middle. The two men hugged in that awkward manly way with a few rounds of back-slapping, but Carey could see the glint of tears in both sets of eyes as they stepped back to their places.

"It's a good place, Rockstead," Declan said gruffly. "Good place to anchor a man's feet. Not so good for anchoring a soul. I've learned that."

"Welcome to the family, Dad." Ryder's voice broke. "The family of God."

CHAPTER TWENTY-FOUR

R yder drew Carey's chair out and seated her. She looked amazing today. Well, she always did, but this November evening she was in her element in a pretty pink dress with gold swirls all over it. Her hair had been swept into an updo that left little wisps around her neck, where a pink cameo dangled from a fine chain inside her square neckline.

"You're beautiful." He settled across from her and grinned at her slight blush. He'd tell her a hundred times a day. It always got a reaction. "Tell me about your necklace. I haven't seen it before." Maybe he shouldn't admit that. Maybe she'd worn it a dozen times and he simply hadn't noticed.

"It was Granny's." Carey fumbled with the clasp behind her neck then she disengaged it and laid it in his hand. "It's a locket."

"A locket?" He angled a questioning look at her.

"Open it."

A closer examination revealed a latch so minuscule he wasn't sure he could get his thick fingers in there, but he managed. The small object opened to reveal two tiny portraits, a man and a woman dressed in old-fashioned garb. "Is this your grandmother?"

"And my grandfather, yes. I don't remember him. He died when I was a baby, but Mom and Laurel and I lived with Granny for a while after the divorce."

"It's a great memento." He studied the images, trying to see a glimpse of Carey in their faces. "I can see why it means so much to you."

"My granny adored antiques. I guess that's why I decorate with them myself."

Ryder nodded. He didn't love her furniture. It wasn't that comfortable, but he had to admit it looked pretty classy. Maybe they could blend styles after they were... He didn't even dare think the word. Not yet.

"She also got me onto reading Regency romances."

He'd seen the old-fashioned covers in her apartment and teased her. That had been a couple of months ago, now.

"I'd like to say there was something more honorable about that time period, but there really wasn't. Those novels highlight the lavish lifestyles of the nobility. They weren't exactly exemplary human beings. I've tried some American history romances, but they're just not that appealing to me. I don't know why."

Ryder would hold that thought.

Ellen Chamberlain stood at the end of their table. "Good evening."

"Mom!" Carey glanced between her mother and Ryder. "Did you know we were coming? Because you don't usually..."

"Of course, I noticed when Ryder made a reservation. I

couldn't let someone else wait on my own daughter and her boyfriend."

Ryder kept his face impassive. He'd had a long talk with Ellen and Frank a couple of weeks ago. It might be antiquated to ask a girl's parents for their blessing, but he knew most of his brothers had done it, and it had smoothed things out between everyone. Might have helped Noah with Taryn's parents if they hadn't eloped. Of course, not everyone's parents were as obnoxious as Taryn's.

Whatever. Not Ryder's problem. His had been wondering if he should pay a visit to the state prison in Deer Lodge and ask to see Jason. He couldn't bring himself to make the drive. Ellen had been horrified he'd even considered it. She was probably right. Jason had abdicated his rights to that sort of honor years ago.

"I'd like to surprise you two this evening," Ellen said. "May I?"

Carey's eyes were wide as they pleaded with Ryder. "Okay?"

"That sounds excellent, Ellen. Frank's in the kitchen? We put ourselves in your capable and talented hands."

"I'll be back with your appetizer." Ellen winked at Ryder as she turned away.

"What was all that about? Last time we were here, my mom was so nasty to you I didn't think we'd ever come back."

"That was months ago. Things change."

"Do they, now?" Her eyebrows angled up.

"You just might have to trust me."

"Trust you?" She tilted her head to one side as she inspected his face.

That was fine. It gave him the chance to study her in return. Once he'd been too bashful to meet her gaze, but not anymore. Now he reveled in the open flirting they shared. The fact they no longer had any secrets between them.

Okay, fine. He had a secret. But he wasn't going to keep it much longer.

Carey looked down and rearranged her silverware before looking back at him. "Ryder, I do trust you. You've earned that confidence over and over."

He stilled her hands against the white linen tablecloth. Was she nervous? Because her hands seemed to tremble. Maybe she could sense the enormity of the evening. Maybe he hadn't been as subtle as he'd hoped.

Was he ready?

More than.

How could Ryder look so casual?

Maybe Carey was imagining things. Either she'd jumped to conclusions about Mom's not only acceptance of Ryder in The Meating Place but her guidance of their meal, which had been excellent. Or, Carey had misjudged Ryder completely, and he was nonchalant because there was nothing special going on.

She'd picked at the appetizer, though it was deserving of full attention. She'd done a little better with the seafood platter. Mom had definitely chosen all Carey's favorites so far. Now they were waiting for dessert.

Where was Ryder taking her next? She had no idea. He'd simply told her to dress up. He'd done the same, wearing a Western-style suit jacket over a crisp baby blue shirt with a bolo tie, with jeans that looked brand new and polished cowboy boots. Yes, she'd checked.

"Enjoying dinner?" Ryder toyed with his water glass.

"Yes, thank you. My stepdad is an excellent chef."

"He is. And a pretty decent human, too."

When had Ryder had occasion to get to know Frank? Carey tried to ask with her eyes, without words, but Ryder didn't seem to catch the question.

Frank approached with two bowls of creme brûlée. He set them on the table and bowed slightly. "Enjoy." Then he stepped back.

Carey picked up her spoon before noticing the mint leaf on top of the caramelized topping. And on top of the leaf...

She gasped and clapped both hands over her mouth. "Ryder!"

But he was kneeling beside her chair and tugging her hands down to her lap. "Caroline Joan Anderson, will you do me the honor of becoming my wife? I love you with everything in me. Will you marry me?"

"Ryder!" She flung her arms around his neck, nearly rocking him off his knees. "Yes! Oh, my goodness, *yes!*"

His arms went about her as their lips met. This was so awkward, her seated, him kneeling. They should just—

Someone coughed. "Told you," came Frank's voice.

Heat roared up her face. They were making out in a fancy restaurant. Well, Ryder had just proposed, but still.

Proposed! And she'd said yes. They were engaged! She was so in love with this man.

He chuckled into her neck, and all she wanted was to kiss him some more. "I love you, Ryder."

Applause went up around them. What, there was more of an audience than Mom and Frank? Carey tore her gaze from her beloved's face and found a small semicircle of friends —

family — around them. Dafne and Blake. Ainsley and Nathaniel.

Ainsley winked and gave her a thumbs-up.

Ryder was still on one knee, holding Carey's hands. She looked down as he slipped a gorgeous ring on her finger. An opal. Wait. She'd seen this ring before.

"Mom?" Her voice squeaked.

"Your granny's." Mom sounded equally emotional. "I've been holding it for you, just hoping you'd marry a man who'd trust me enough to ask what you'd like. You found a good one, sweetie."

"Thanks." Carey tried for more words, but they garbled and choked in her throat.

Ryder's thumb wiped an errant tear from her cheek. "You okay, sweetheart? Did I make a mistake?"

She buried her face into his shoulder and gave up trying to hold back the tears. "It's perfect. I can't believe how perfect. That's why I'm crying."

"Okay." His hands soothed her back until she'd pulled herself together. Then he eased back enough to look her in the eye. "You sure?"

"Positive." She probably looked a mess, like she'd been eating chocolate or something. Dessert. There was a perfect creme brûlée or two on the table. Frank was a wizard with those things, and if they waited too long, the crispy topping would start to soften.

Did she care, right here, right now? Yeah, she did. Suddenly she was starving. She could eat that whole meal over again.

Seemingly satisfied she was, indeed, fine, Ryder rounded the table. His two brothers and their wives offered congratulations then wandered back to their own table across the restaurant. Mom and Frank stepped away.

Just the two of them, once again.

They were engaged to be married! They'd have dinner together every night. She'd cook. Or he would. Or they'd get takeout. Where would they live? Would they build near his brothers' down on the bend? She and her best friend, Ainsley, would be sisters!

Maybe Carey was too excited to eat dessert, after all.

"Ryder?"

His warm, loving gaze met hers across the little table. "Yes?"

"Thank you for trusting me with your heart."

Ryder's eyes darkened. "It's my honor, and I don't take it lightly. Also, same to you."

Carey's heart was full.

EPILOGUE

Always the bridesmaid, never the bride.

That would forever be Stephanie Simpson's destiny. This spring day was bad enough. At least she'd never had designs on Ryder Cavanagh... or any of his brothers, honestly. She'd only had eyes for Eli Bryson for the past several years, and stupid her had walked right in on him proposing to Harper Satterfield on Valentine's Day. One year to the day since Eli had first asked Stephanie out.

But she was over that. Mostly. She'd dated John a few times but hadn't let her parents know. They definitely wouldn't have approved, but it didn't matter. She'd known John wasn't her forever guy. Did one exist? Probably not. Not a truly good man like Eli.

Or, apparently, Ryder, but there were no more Cavanagh brothers.

She should have opened her eyes a few years ago and realized Eli would never love her back the way she loved him. Or, maybe it hadn't been love. Maybe love was just a sappy romantic notion embraced by people like Carey Anderson-soon-to-be-Cavanagh.

If anyone loved the idea of old-fashioned romance, it was Carey. Stephanie had borrowed a few Regency romances from her to see what all the hype was about, but she didn't quite get it.

Carey had laughed and said one day she'd meet the right guy, and it would all make sense.

Stephanie doubted it. Her parents might be a team, the perfect church elder and his demure wife, but if they'd ever had a swoony moment, it had passed on by in a few seconds.

Dad ruled the roost, and Mom didn't seem to mind. Stephanie wasn't going to be that kind of wife.

Ha. At this rate, she wasn't going to be a wife at all. Today she was one of Carey's bridesmaids. In August, she'd be Harper's. Yes, while her rival married Eli.

Being a good little girl hadn't gotten her anywhere. Maybe she should live a little.

"Are you ready?" Carey asked.

Laurel and Ainsley gathered closer as Carey prayed over the four of them before they walked down the aisle.

Stephanie wished her faith was as strong as Carey's.

Not only that, but her friend was gorgeous in that Victorian-inspired gown. Or Regency. One of those eras Stephanie still couldn't keep straight. Maybe because she didn't care enough.

The list of things she cared *enough* about was getting shorter and shorter.

Was it so wrong to want to be loved for herself? Just because Stephanie Simpson was an amazing woman? Maybe she needed to believe that was true before she could expect someone else to. Because, while she'd mostly convinced herself she was okay with Harper and Eli's engagement, what her heart really craved was for someone to love her that way. That much.

It was easy, in retrospect, to see what she'd been blind to for so long: that Eli had never loved her. Oh, he'd tried. He'd been kind and respectful. He'd kissed her, but there'd been no passion.

Stephanie took her place as the first bridesmaid to walk the aisle. The church was decorated in pink roses. Wasn't that so Carey? But Ryder didn't seem to mind. He stood tall and strong at the front of the church next to... Eli.

She willed herself not to trip over her own feet. She'd dreamed of walking the aisle toward Eli, but not like this. Not when he was the officiant, and she was a bridesmaid.

Branson deWitt stood on Ryder's left side, then Nathaniel, then Blake.

If forever being a bridesmaid wasn't bad enough, she was paired with a married man. She couldn't even flirt with him — not that she was experienced at teasing, so it was just as well.

She had a role to play here today. Then another in August. Then, somewhere, somehow, she was going to figure out what she needed to do going forward. For herself.

A NOTE...

Dear Stephanie,

I'm sorry you are still pining over Eli. Or, if not over him exactly, over the perfect image you held of the two of you together. I'm sorry you can't be happier for him and Harper and for Carey and Ryder.

But, I want you to know that I see you. I feel your struggle with worthiness. I absorb your need to be loved.

Please hold on, Stephanie. Don't do anything rash. I promise there's a romance out there for you. It's coming soon.

Be patient. Hold the faith.

Your loving author, Valerie

Dear Reader,

I hope you have loved the journey of the sixth and final Cavanagh brother to find his bride. I also hope you have cheered for Kathryn and Declan throughout these stories and are happy to see them moving forward together.

But, what if there was more?

Could I interest you in a series epilogue? *Keep Me in Your Vows, Cowboy* is a short story available to subscribers of my biweekly newsletter. Sign up here! https://valeriecomer.-com/connect/subscribe-cavanagh/

If you're already a subscriber, there's a link in my most

recent email for you to download your copy. I appreciate you so much!

If you're eager to continue the journey of cowboys near Jewel Lake, may I welcome you to the Sweet River Ranch series? Stephanie Simpson finds her happily-ever-after in *A Surprise Wedding for the Cowboy*, and I hope you'll enjoy getting to know the Sullivan grandsons as they learn to work together to build on their grandfather's legacy. Chances are good you'll catch a glimpse of a Cavanagh or two in those pages, as well.

And, if you missed Harper and Eli's story (in which Stephanie found herself on the outside), you can find that in *Amethyst Attraction*, part of the Pot of Gold Geocaching Romance series.

All that and more! Thanks for reading.

Valerie

ACKNOWLEDGMENTS

Thanks so much to all my readers who've loved my cowboys — the Delgados, the Carmichaels, the Havilands, and now, the Cavanaghs. Stay tuned for another Montana Ranches Christian Romance series coming soon with the Sullivans!

Always, always, thanks to my fellow author and friend, Elizabeth Maddrey. She prods, cheers, and commiserates as needed, then offers helpful brainstorming and critiques.

My amazing editor, Nicole, has been with me from the beginning. I am so thankful for her!

I'm also grateful for the Christian Indie Authors Facebook group and my sister bloggers at Inspy Romance. These folks make a difference in my life every single day. I'm thrilled to walk beside them as we tell stories for Jesus!

Thank you to my Facebook friends, followers, street team, and reader group members for prayers, encouragement, and great fellowship. If you'd like to join other readers who love my stories, please find us at Valerie Comer: Readers Group.

Thanks to my husband, Jim, whose love for me never fails and who encourages me in every endeavor. Thanks to my kids, their spouses, and my wonderful grandkids for cheering me on. To them, having an author for a mom/grandma is "normal." Imagine that!

All my love and gratitude goes to Jesus, the One who is my vision, the High King of Heaven, the lord of my heart. Thank You. A thousand times, thank You.

ABOUT VALERIE COMER

Valerie Comer's life on a small farm in western Canada provides the seed for stories of contemporary Christian romance. Like many of her characters, Valerie grows much of her own food and is active in the local foods movement as well as her church. She only hopes her imaginary friends enjoy their happily-ever-afters as much as she does hers, shared with her husband, adult kids, and adorable grandkids.

Valerie is a *USA Today* bestselling author and a two-time Word Award winner. She writes engaging characters, strong communities, and deep faith into her green clean romances.

To find out more, visit her website at www.valeriecomer.com, where you can read her blog, explore her many links, and sign up for her email newsletter, where you will find news, giveaways, deals, book recommendations and more.

You can also find Valerie blogging with other authors of Christian contemporary romance at Inspy Romance.